MY OLD AGE, A MENU I MUST CHOOSE

MY OLD AGE, A MENU I MUST CHOOSE

Dr. José de Jesús Valencia Rodríguez

My old age, a menu I must choose
Derechos reservados
© Dr. José de Jesús Valencia Rodríguez

Primera edición 2019

RDA: 03-2019-013011319 1900-01
ISBN: 978-607-9104-02-3

Foto de Portada: Kristen Perreira
Impreso en México

MY OLD AGE, A MENU I MUST CHOOSE
Or… "how to live many years with dignity and quality and not get old in the attempt".

Prologue

In 2010, a little bit after I turned 60, and when I presented the book "Living Without Aging XII" (or in Spanish, "Vivir Sin Envejecer XII"), I wrote a prologue that I, and several other people, considered different. I will transcribe it and afterwards, I will share my current, acute and deep observations and experiences regarding… aging:

> *It is very odd. The first memories I have of my father are from when he was 30 years old… he seemed to me quite old; in other words, almost a very old person.*
>
> *Really old was my grandma Tana (Atanasia), maybe because of her way to live looking for salvation, or for the time she spent in church; my grandma Chicha (Narcisa), despite being more or less the same age as the former, she did not strike me as someone "very old", since she travelled very often, coming from Mexico City to Guadalajara to visit us very frequently, always smelled like "Ramillete de Novia", a perfume that existed back then, she tied boxes, packed the clothes and ran through the train station, since she travelled in the Pullman coach, or in the bus some other times, especially in "Tres Estrellas de Oro" line, which no longer exists.*
>
> *Grandma Tana told me, every time she had the chance to, that if I sinned, I would burn in the "eternal flames of*

hell" for eternity (I did not fully understand the concept of "eternity", but that really terrified me).

Grandma Chicha prepared the most delicious coffee with milk I have memories of; I spent significantly long periods of time with her, first in Mexico City, then in Zitacuaro, and finally in Ciudad Guzman, since, my uncles' jobs (her sons) required them to move around, and they took her with them. I still have the image of the cup in my mind: it was pretty big, by the way, and had a very small handle according to my appreciation, when compared to the rest of it. It had three parallel golden lines that went around the body of the cup. She poured the coffee, which still had some particles of ground coffee, while a steam column invited me to carefully drink the first sip.

They both died under my care in one of the resting homes I have operated: they both died at old age. I cannot remember their ages right now.

Now my father is 84 and does not seem to be an old man, because he is very active, flirty, incredibly religious, and supporter of PAN, a Mexican political party, up to his very core. Nevertheless, the passing of the years has taken some of his height.

My mother died in 1999, October the 2nd, exactly two months before FIL'Abuelos was presented for the first time. I still miss her. She didn't seem an elderly woman when she died either.

There are things that are very clear to me precisely now that I have reached the old age (freakin' expression that was surely invented by someone that was an old guy from the day he was born).

When I turned 15, I felt like... an adult... hahaha! (back then, when one reached that age, one stopped being considered as an adolescent and started being conside-

red as an adult): truth is that only for knowing the truth about some "secrets" that remained hidden during my past years, I started feeling almost like an "adult". I will let you in on some of those "secrets": baby Jesus (or Santa Claus in the US) does not bring the toys in Christmas Eve. Saying "pregnancy" is not a "bad word"; babies are not brought by the stork. The reason behind women peeing sitting down and men standing up hit me around two years later... maybe three.

I laugh at my naivety now.

Nevertheless, some changes started happening in my anatomy; some hair here and there, and I started using bigger sizes of shirts, shoes and pants.

The years went by and more "secrets" started seeing the light little by little, some thanks to the explanation, especially, of my mother, but most thanks to my classmates. A couple of times, I received the clarification or lesson from a girl that was younger than me, but of course, way more "awaken" than yours truly.

Despite of the above, I did not feel neither an adult, nor a child, nor a teenager... only me, Pepe Valencia, and of course, in several occasions I had to pretend to be familiar with this or that subject with my friends, who were not only familiar with the subject: they dominated it!

This thing we call time has passed by. I have measured it in years because of the influence of everyone and everything that surrounds me. However, I feel exactly the same as when I turned 15, only with a little more experience.

My dreams still go on, my concerns still go on, the fear of losing a loved one remain within me, I laugh my tears out and guffaw at everything the coyote goes *through when trying to catch the roadrunner, and at the adventures of Snoopy and Charlie and the gang; I still love cucumber with lemon and salt, and bolillo (a kind of Mexican bread roll that can only be cooked in Guadalajara, AKA "birote"), stuffed in a cup with sugar, eating it spoonful by spoonful: using glasses to read and watch gray hairs in my head has not been an obstacle for the above to continue happening; then, where or from what point have I gotten older? Only because I can hear my knees grind a little bit when I do a squat or because there are some small brown stains in the back of my hands? Just because I have three loved grandchildren? Is this really being old?*

Well, I don't accept it: if I qualify myself as an old person because of what I asked at the last part of the previous paragraph, then I am not getting older: I am <u>graduating</u>. My body is filling with characteristics that are attributed to the old age: my eyes do not see as well as they used to, I have more and more gray hairs, I am losing some hair, my face shows a thousand wrinkles, I need to go to the bathroom more often during the nights, but I definitely do not feel old. And beware! Don't think that I am in denial! It is totally clear to me that the human being I claim to be is not formed or represented by this bag of skin, muscles (a little bit), brain (even less) and bones; it is formed by what is inside my body, and of course, that one does not get old! It grows, it graduates... or I grow, I graduate, I learn, I enjoy... I cry!

And so then, I welcome this stage of my life in which I keep the flavor or grandma Chicha's coffee in my mouth, the flavor of what I lived when I was 15, my graduation as doctor: I keep the child I have always been and that I tried to hide thousands of times to avoid people looking into my interior; now I could not care less to wear a Snoopy pin in my blazer when presenting in a conference or wearing socks with his figure. I still believe in magic, in dreams and fantasies. I still believe that there are beautiful people and that the bad guys are not so bad, but they respond to the punches they have taken in life.

Now it's my turn. I have devoted the last 11 years of my life to support my dear authors of old age in every sense; now it's my turn to place some of the lines that dance in my mind when I wonder, am I an old man?

I hope, dear reader, that the contents of this book reinforces your concepts of maturity, attitude, growing old, childhood, and of course, love. Love for everything that is alive and everything that is not.

Pepe Valencia.

60 years of living: of Living Without Aging.

Looks good, doesn't it? Well, I still agree with everything I wrote there, and so, I have a greater desire of telling you that the usage of phrases such as "golden age", "age of splendor", "the beautiful winter of life", "light of winter", "sunset and glamour", and other are not more than crappy euphemisms! Yes, euphemisms! The old age that the Mexican these days live is NOT "golden", nor is it winter. That stupid idea of considering us calendars or seasons of the year! Or what I think is even worse, as Vicente Fox says, "adults in their splendor" ... Adults in their splendor, adults in their schmendor! BUT we are not *adults of old age* either... or disabled, or someone who people should pity, or someone that should be stuffed with medicines. However (what does "however" mean anyway? I use this word and I will have to look it up in the dictionary to correctly define it, but in the meantime, I will carry on caressing the keys of my computer with my emotions), here it goes: however, there are plenty of factors, situations, experiences we live that plain and simply make those phrases sound just like bullshit (making use of my poetic license, of course... not to say any stupid remark).

Does it seem like "golden" or "splendor" to have to get up from 1 to 5 times to the bathroom sometimes, whether you are a woman or a man, and come back to bed with the "treacherous drop" (which after some years becomes the "treacherous stream", in case you're a man) right there...? And what about having to look for your glasses just not to miss the toilet? Or having to sit down to pee? Or having to take 20 or more seconds to get out of bed before starting your day, looking for your glasses, putting your dental bridge or your dentures so that, when you pass in front of the mirror (with your glasses on, naturally) you don't look so... old? What happens in your mind when you look at a chronologically young person, whether it is a man or a woman, showing those attributes, either a huge set of pecs and/or succulent bosoms, desirable behind and without any wrinkle in all of his or her anatomy? Of course you would crave for a bite, a grab or a rub of all of the above they so glamorously show off and... you settle for an "ocular orgasm"! Allow me to be a bit more aggressive! What if when you run into a girl you tremendously like at a bar, and maybe, thinking you have plenty of money (or are you going to say you look like a Richard Gere?), you nervously buy her a drink, and she finally accepts to go to your place (maybe driven by gerontophilia), and on the way there you notice that you have run out of Viagra? "Panic" is the word that describes everything that leaps from one side to the other in your head!

Woman: what happens in your head when despite your trendy makeup, paid for by this month's pension of your late husband, you go to a get together or a party and you are asked about your age? And even worse, if they say something like: "I have a friend that sells an anti-wrinkle cream that I think you would...". Or, what do you feel when suddenly, when coughing, or maybe when doing a little effort when pulling the chair to the table, or when you soundly guffaw because of a joke some friend told, you notice that a little stream of pee escapes?

Can you imagine the name a 77-year-old woman from "Grupo Plenitud" Queretaro gave to the male members? The Dead Birds Club! And, do you know what one of the guys named the group of women? Jurassic Park!

I have had the idea to have a bar and call it "The G Spot", but not because of what you are thinking... because it would be the Geriatric Spot!

Hundreds and hundreds of plastic surgeons receive hefty monetary incomes from women (and men too!) for the application of Botox, esthetic surgeries, application of implants, etc., etc.

I am going to take the liberty to share a little joke, without the intention of offending any woman. What do older women have between their breasts that younger women don't? A belly button!

Wow!... Another wow! I once had one of these experiences when I took a girl for breakfast to a fancy restaurant, and I got there a little bit earlier. I took a bite out of the delicious bread that a beautiful eyed, cute smile and kindly flirty waitress had left on my table. I spread some butter over it, it took it to my mouth and while chewing it, the "permanent" dental bridge I had in my mouth came off! Sheez! In that precise moment, my guest was being walked to the table by the cute waitress; I was not able to say anything to either one of them at the moment. I smiled like stupid, and with my index and thumb fingers I asked to be excused, ran to the bathroom, and since it was a fancy restaurant, I asked to the guy at the bathroom (I don't know the name of the function of the guy that is dressed nicely at the entrance of the men's room) if he had super glue! For my absolute and immense happiness, he DID have some; I got into the bathroom, took the lid off the bottle, put ONE drop of the darned magic glue in the bridge, dried the spot it should be on the best I could and placed it... Sheez! There it is! But now I also had two of my fingers super glued to the bridge and to my gum! Yes... laugh, laugh as I do now! Like lightning, Mr. Nicely Dressed Guy at the Bathroom brought a bottle of the oil used for baby's behinds along with acetone. After a couple of endless minutes, and thanks to Divine intervention (I think), at some point, my fingers were finally released from where they were romantically adhered.

Oh, yes! In case you're wondering, I DID check that I did not take the dental bridge between my fingers!

Upon coming back to the table, I still had the flavor of the super glue in my taste buds, while my fingers still had whitish stains left behind by the freakin' glue. The eggs Benedict I ordered tasted like Play-Doh the rest of our date! I also couldn't help being afraid of the stupid "permanent" bridge coming off again and becoming part of the breakfast.

... Mr. Nicely Dressed Guy at the Bathroom charged me 60 pesos for the freakin' super glue... but did not charge me for the baby oil I had used!

NO, my purpose with these lines is not to make you believe that the old age is a tragedy, or that is better to never reach this age, nooooo! My purpose is to "sow" in you –whatever your age or gender may be—the n-e-e-d of **planning** your old age, starting at this **p-r-e-c-i-s-e m-o-m-e-n-t**. When YOU plan intelligently that stage of life every human being goes through, accepting that it is one of the most absolute stages of life, you will be able to live each day of your existence in a more *elective* way, and not only as the *consequence* of having lived many years, freeing you in the process of *depending* on somebody else and accepting your choices, whatever they may be. This means: planning your whole life, particularly your old age. This is pure *gerontoprophylaxis*: it is planning and writing every page of the book of your life beforehand, knowing that there might be some changes to it and that you will be in charge of doing corrections or adjustments, thus, the real sense of living alive will be written by you: NOBODY ELSE.

In these pages, I don't want to *deny* the processes that come with old age; I am not seeking to "scent" the blows that those –us, I correct—who are in this stage of life perceive: I don't want to invite you to jump up and down in joy because you are already 60, 70, 80, 90 or more years old either (please don't… we don't want a broken leg in the process). What I want to do is for you to become aware; *invite* you to turn your head towards this stage of life; invite you first and foremost, and in the best of the cases to accept that you will become old in a blink of time, but that you need to take the decisions AND actions that make your life a canvas in which you are the main actor, and that no one, absolutely no one besides you should add strokes that deform the work of art your life is, as long as you are the artist.

DEDICATION

I want to dedicate this work to several human beings that are VERY significant in my life for diverse reasons:

To my daughter and son, as they are now part of that group of human beings I call "teachers", since at this age I have understood that children were not given to us to teach them something, but to learn from them. Sons, thank you for your teachings!

Of course, to my loved grandchildren, Mateo, Alexa, Vicky and Sofia, who despite their young age have accepted that I am geographically far from them to pursue my dreams: thank you for your love and for the privilege of being your grandpa.

To my wife Norma, who has learnt to respect my function in this world, and maintains her love to me, in spite of my lack of attentions she legitimately deserves, only for my being immersed in this idea of sowing a quality way of life for the old aged in Mexico and for those who might want to take advantage of the message. Norma, thank you: I love you.

Definitively, my eternal gratitude and love to my dear Rafa Lonngi, who sowed a great deal of what I now practice and offer to you.

To everyone that supports me in this wonderful adventure: Karen, Eliza, Irais, Nicolas, his daughter Renata, Paty, Gaby, Alex, Sarahi, Mary, Roxana, Mony Urdapilleta and Claudia, without whom, I affirm it, it would not be possible to continue with the mutual dream of spreading the concept of "Living Without Aging", or *gerontoprophylaxis*, as they have several times dispelled me from the desire of giving up.

And to you, who grants me the privilege of being a part of your learning and, believe it or not, mine too, when reading this more-than-work, the object through which I have longed to share what I have learned from my real teachers, with the desire of your life having a better quality and less, much less pain than the one they have gone through. My gratitude when placing before my dreams your fertile land for your old age to have the flower of quality and dignity, which are one of the main objectives of my life.

INTRODUCTION

Sayings are "sparks of wisdom" contained within a few words. *"You will pay for the excesses of your youth during your old age"* is in no way an exception and seeks to confer that everything you do, not do, besides mistakes and every type of experiences you go through during the stage of life we call "youth", will surely be paid for in the other stage of life we call "old age".

Obviously, I'm referring to the *chronological* stage of our lives, given that there are "old" people that are 40 years old, and "young" people that are 95 years old, but this is not what we are going to speak about in this work, but the really fundamental aspects needed to having a quality life once we get to 60, 70, 80, 90 and older, using every experience that my teachers (the old aged, who I have had the honor to look after during my life) have passed on to me.

The above is represented by a big word that I don't even remember having "invented" myself, which merit I don't claim, but that represents what we *should* do during our lives, -I repeat- to have an old age with quality until the last moment. The word is *gerontoprophylaxis*.

Its meaning is, *preparing in every sense possible to design ourselves our old age, seeking to live the most dignity and quality of living possible without the dependencies that currently exist in almost every culture in the world. Simply put:* **to live alive and to die alive***, but based on* **our** *early decisions essentially.*

During my professional practice, I have gone through various stages, from caring for my patients (now I don't like that word, since patience is a characteristic needed for the medical professional, whichever his branch of specialty may be, and not needed by the person –the human being—that is going through a health problem or situation and that comes to the doctor to be oriented). As I was saying, from caring for my patients (which I now call *teachers*, but to avoid confusions I will continue to refer to them throughout this work as "patients"); once again I jump back on my train of thought, and I used to assist those patients simply as clinical cases, as sick people, and even worse: as the numbers that were printed on the cover of their clinical records, or as their diagnostic: the one with arthritis, the one with Alzheimer... etc. As I kept on learning from them and after researching and comparing our culture and the process of getting old with that of other countries and also other moments of our history, it has become clear to me that we are a bunch of greenhorns regarding the attention of patients, especially the old aged patients!

After a while, I understood the *necessary* factors for any individual to be satisfied with his life and his surroundings at any age.

This work is based on the investigations and conclusions that up to this moment I have gathered and that surely will soon increase, given the "evolution" we are going through.

When speaking about these factors that I will shortly mention and that if followed carefully, constantly and closely, then we would be establishing the mentioned gerontoprophylaxis; that is to say, executing the steps that in a not so detailed way I will describe throughout this work, and that will surely be the points or factors to have a full, happy, healthy old age, and without the years being a decisive factor for it to be successful in every way possible.

To increase your interest in these points, I'll have you know that somebody that has gathered all of these factors in his life, whatever his or her age may be, is a healthy individual, both mentally as physically (let's understand that one is consequence of the other, please) and that the word "sickness" is not part of his vocabulary or sounds strange to him or her whenever somebody says: "I'm sick", since once that he has integrated these elements, he is a strong being in every sense, without the need of medications or treatments: *he is his own preventive healer* if it is needed.

The already mentioned factors which I had referred to in so many moments are:

1.- Health

2.- Nutrition

3.- Identity

4.- Sense of Belonging

5.- Goals

6.- Material possessions, satisfactory finances

7.- Socialization

8.- Affectivity

9.- Sexuality

10.- Spirituality

11.- Autonomy

12.- My five wishes

In this moment, I want to let you know that I will be as honest and open while expressing all that I wish for the life of the old aged in your life to improve, but mainly your own, whether it is in the present time or in the future, when you become old aged: I will not contain myself. I will however not try to be offensive: I will be crystal clear so that there is no question or confusions regarding everything I want to share with you, which is what I have obtained from the life of hundreds and hundreds of old aged people I have had the privilege to assist up to their partings. I hope that it makes you live in the best way possible, without having to pay in your old age the mistakes or excesses of your young age.

Let's move on to the description of each one of them: please note, dear reader, that my greatest desire is to sow the seed in the greatest quantity of people possible so that they don't live the habits and customs we drag from many preceding generations; that we may not depend blindly on the concepts of "sickness" or "medicines and treatments", where we were told that stepping barefoot on the floor would cause us tonsillitis or pneumonia, where the word of the doctor is the law, where ignorance on what follows death is necessarily horrible according to the "sins we have committed", where the most valuable thing you can do is fulfill the demands and the customs of a group we call "society" and forget about being ourselves, pursuing what we were given, and that represents a principle that is truly superior to all of those burdens that prevent us from, as I mentioned: **live alive and... die alive.**

CLARIFICATION

Given the freakishly hard nature of the first three points, Health, Nutrition and Identity, I will leave them for the end to be able to elaborate as much as possible. Therefore, the first point I will expand on will be the *Sense of Belonging.*

FIRST PART

SENSE OF BELONGING

Ever since most of the inhabitants of our prehistoric world decided one day to leave behind their nomadic behavior and find a place where they could remain most of the time and as comfortable as possible, maybe conditioned by some factors such as the presence of water, nice climate, easily attainable food, protection from the risks that existed at that time, the human being became sedentary: he established his home. I have to mention that this applies to every living being: plants and animals, and even inanimate beings, but this is a subject that corresponds to other branches of science and not because of that it stops being wonderful.

Once that a place to live had been defined, head of families of that time went out to obtain their meals, reach agreements with other people or social groups, went out to hunt or to collect fruits and then came back the same day or some days after to their house... their home... the place where they belonged.

The word **"arraigo"** (or **"belonging"** in English) is formed by Latin roots and means "action of putting down roots", since their lexical components are: *ad-* (towards) and *radix* (roots), apart from the suffix *-icus, igo* (which means "relative to").

This is, putting down roots, or feeling that one belongs to a specific geographical space.

This explains the reason behind such a delicious feeling when coming back home after what we considered our best vacations ever: we come back to the place we belong, we come back home, where we feel that sense of belonging. Once home, we enjoy or bedroom, our pillow, our favorite corners: we enjoy the place we feel we belong to!

The value this factor represents in the human being is very important, since when lacking this sense of belonging, one feels unprotected, without a place to go to and really rest. Something similar happens when we spend the night in another house, or even in another bedroom: when we wake up we feel like we don't belong there, strangers and somewhat disoriented for some seconds, and then we remember where or why we are there, and until then we recover our peace.

The sense of belonging provides us with the security and wellbeing and does not only apply to one's home, but to one's neighborhood or usual surroundings, to one's city, town or ranch, especially to one's country; I will again reference the moment you are back from a trip, whether it is a business or a pleasure trip; as soon as we see the lights of our city or of the place we belong to, we feel happier.

The feeling of belonging also applies to the objects that are in our home, such as our favorite couch, the bed and the place we occupy in it, the place where we eat our meals, and plenty of things more. Even while being home, if we switch the place where we eat or sleep, we go through some not so comfortable moments, that change as soon as we go back to our spots. Try this and you will see, is your husband easily willing to sleep on the opposite side of the bed? Do you feel good when your wife asks you to sleep on the couch, which, as comfortable as it may be, it is NOT the place where you feel belonging? ... I must clarify that I don't want to speak about subjects related to the reason you were sent to sleep on the couch, as I am no psychologist, nor I am a couple counselor (...). Simply, modify the places you are accustomed to and you will notice the discomfort this causes to you.

Up to this moment, I am sure that you have it completely understood. Therefore, the real value of this factor out of the 12 I mentioned at the beginning is applied when an individual reaches the stage of the old age and their relatives, in an effort of making his or her life easier, decide (in most of the cases, all of the family members and the doctor or doctors are the ones who take the decision, *instead* of the elder, may it be the father, the mother or the grandparent...); as I was saying, they decide to take care of him or her by taking him or her to their homes, spending in each one of them periods of time that vary according to the possibilities of each one of the members of the family.

I know that in this moment you are already sensing what I want to say: they modify their sense of belonging! With the best and the most loving of the intentions of each one of the members of the family, they affect one of the essential factors needed for the wellbeing of a human being, in this case, the elders of the family. Without noticing, they are stripping away the wellbeing they have been living during who knows how many years: they give him beds, furniture, nightlamps, chairs or couches, places to eat and everything, everything is totally different to those things he was used to for maybe decades! What or which are the reactions that you think that may result from these actions? I totally agree that this is one of the ways to support them and care for them, however, I think that it is very important to point out, in its whole measure and value, what the absence of sense of belonging causes to them.

The worst comes when he *is taken* to Enriqueta's house (the daughter), and a month later to Gerardo's house (the son), where grandpa spends only two weeks, because Gerardo travels very frequently, and he would be leaving his father alone; then he *is moved* to Lolita's house, since she is the spinster of the family and has most of her time available to care for him or her. Can you imagine the conflicts this means to them in their mind and the consequences that this implies in both their physical and mental health? Eating, sleeping, sitting, standing up, going to the bathroom... living! (actually, half-living) in different homes, eating different food, with different schedules, with different personalities... different conditions in every way, and none of those conditions chosen by the elderly!

Result: they become more propense for that condition many call "sickness" to present. Or... what would happen to you?

Other families decide to take them to an old people's home, nursing home, residence for the elder, "happy" home for the grandpas, with some even using the names of saints to make them seem more compassionate and loving for their residents. This decision, in our Mexican culture, is not an easy one to take, and represents, in most of the cases, an important difficulty. The difficulty I am talking about when they decide to do this is the belief that they are doing it to "get rid" of their old relatives, to which I irrefutably say to you: that is a horrible lie. It may be true that this happens very frequently, and where the financial factor also plays a very important part, this could be the best choice.

In a nursing home –let's stick to this phrase–, they receive in one place the same quality of food, apart from the fact that they are appropriate and balanced for their personal needs. They also receive the same attentions provided by the same people in a permanent environment; they receive medical supervision and when the condition of any of them is altered, relatives are immediately notified. In the homes of the relatives, in plenty of times it is almost impossible to totally fulfill the needs of the old aged, and if they put their effort in doing it, it is very likely for the lifestyle of the family seeking to do so to be altered.

No, it's not that I am in favor or against the nursing homes: I'm in favor of the quality of life of the old aged AND all of his relatives, since "when the elder becomes sick, the whole family becomes sick too".

Continuing with the subject of the nursing homes, I ask the following question: are they a need? Are they a *necessary evil?* Are they really as bad as people say they are?

I will share what as per my way of thinking, after almost 40 years (this year being 2017) of looking after old aged in nursing homes in different parts of Mexico, and some in USA, I consider what needs to exist in that nursing home or institution for the elder so that if you do it, you take the best decision and benefits every member of the family (I am talking about the facilities, services, green spaces, ventilation, food, staff, philosophy, activities, etc.), but before, I want to ask this question to you: who is your priority: your spouse? Your sons? Your parents? Your grandparents? Your job? Perhaps yourself? If you responded that your parents, grandparents or spouse, I need to tell you that you are mistaken or confused. The priority has to be you always and above all, since if you don't provide to yourself what is necessary for you, you will not be able to provide or satisfy the needs of every loved one.

Now, another question: who *has* to be the priority after you? Definitely not your parents or grandparents! It is your spouse, and then your sons! Then, your job, and then your home! Otherwise, how could you have the tranquility if you alter the order of these roles? I know plenty of cases of distraught parents because his daughter left home with her boyfriend, or because his son started using drugs, or because the spouse is cheating on him or her, and, do you know why? Because you gave more importance to other members of the family than the one who deserved it the most! You modified roles! You changed *priorities!* I know about plenty of marriages that are broken up, or sons that once mature reproach their parents for their scarce or lack of attention, time and love they received from them during their childhood because they were busy looking after their parents or grandparents who one day died! In the meantime, their sons were facing their lives without their required support.

There is another factor that is also a mistake and that has to be considered to decide to look after the elder at home: the role situation. Your father or mother *will always* need to be so, and you their son or daughter. Therefore, when they become your children because of the cares you are providing to them and you their mother or father, some situations will be generated in which you feel you have the right to reprehend them and maybe even punish them, or beg them to eat their food or take their medications, and there will be times when you will let them manipulate you, yes! Aware or not, they develop an unimaginable ability to manipulate and complain about ailments that don't even exist, so that they can get more attention from you, behaving like kids with tantrums and whims.

At this point, you may be involved in a series of conflicts that will surely make you sick and you will make this key principle come true: *"the carer wears out faster than the caree"*.

Another point: the attentions that are provided to the loved ones at home, whether it is the grandparents or the parents, are based in feelings, and not in knowledge or experience, since suddenly you feel the urge to look after them, and the first thing that hits your mind is to satisfy the needs that *you think* they have, based on what would make you feel better. I call this "the sweater syndrome", as the sweater is the garment mom makes her son wear when she feels cold, and asks him to take it off when she feels hot. This is how we care for the elders in the family, because we believe or suppose that is what they need. This is how you satisfy needs that are not theirs, but your assumptions and hence, not precisely what they need.

Even another point: you will not be able to avoid caring for them, and in plenty of moments of the day having guilty feelings when asking yourself if you are giving them the best, or what is most convenient for them, and you will not be able to go to the movies, enjoy a dinner with your spouse or family, go out with friends, and if you do, you will spend the night continuously calling to check on them. What I point out insistently and with plenty of concern is that you think that while they are out of your "shelter", something bad might happen to them, and you will carry the sense of guilt for days, weeks, or your whole life. Given the latter, I reiterate another one of the phrases I use in some conferences: *"the worst caregiver or therapist is the relative"*, as he will care for his old ones precisely because of his fear to live those feelings, and not to fulfill his elder's needs, who will undoubtedly not receive what they need AND deserve. I will illustrate it somewhat strongly inviting you to ask yourself the following question: "And if they die or something bad happens to them while I'm not around, what could alleviate my pain and guilty feelings?".

Now I ask to you: what about your life?

Let's rest for a while.

With joy I share with you what in my opinion has to have and offer a nursing home for your loved one to receive dignity and quality of life during this stage of his life and until the end:

A nursing home or residence for the elder is an institution where people who suffer from certain diseases, besides being old, are taken, since, due to certain situations it is not possible to provide them with the attentions they need at home. This constitutes a real solution, as it excellently alleviates the tension in the family and the quality of life of the elder is better, since he receives those attentions from specialized personnel.

If you decide to take your father or your grandfather to one of these institutions, YOU MUST be aware of the following:

What characteristics must these institutions have? What activities should they offer? Do they really provide what they offer in their publicity? Is the attending staff really properly trained? Vocation? Are the services provided congruent with the price? Do you have any way of confirming that the loved one you have taken to one of these institutions is not victim of abuse or mistreatment in any of its ways? Do you know what kind of food they receive?

An institution of this kind is NOT a closet where you go put your old aged in and is left alone seeing life pass by, or placed in a bed or in front of a television all day long. It is SO MUCH more.

In a very general way, I will mention what MUST be offered and done in these geriatric centers:

1.- They must be architectonically adequate. This is, facilitate and provide security to the residents when moving or being moved throughout all of its areas.

2.- The staff in charge of taking care of the elderly MUST receive continuous training and also have a VERY important characteristic: VOCATION.

3.- You have the right to receive periodic reports regarding the condition of your loved one, as well as the right of verifying the veracity of such reports with the doctor of your choice.

4.- You must have the freedom to visit them in every area of the institution and the freedom to verify that the medications, the food and the services are really provided.

5.- You have to understand that these institutions are certainly a business, but NOT a real estate business, or a restaurant: it is a business where *services* that dignify and improve the quality of the residents' life are provided, and you need to be sure of this because one of the residents is your loved one!

6.- Your loved one SHOULD NOT be taken care of with pity, but with compassion, love for the service, humanism, warmth, sensibility and of course, experience: he being treated as a kid or as a mentally challenged person only shows lack of professionalism and knowledge. The *philosophy of service* provided in that place should be only **one** based on the mentioned points.

7.- You have the right to take an external doctor to see your loved one, same as nurses, caregivers, equipment, without no one at the institution preventing you from doing so.

8.- You must have internet access to communicating and observing the activities that take place in the institution (video cameras, Skype, etc.).

10.- They MUST be trained to care for the needs of their residents when they are in a terminal situation, both from a palliative and a thanatological point of view, alleviating the physical and emotional pain of your loved ones as well as the emotional pain and the grief management of the whole family until the last moment.

The above are only some points I present to you with the purpose of making you think if the attention your loved one, who is resident of one of these institutions anywhere in the world, receives. Otherwise, you ought to take measures so that he receives the quality of life he deserves.

The concept of **sense of belonging** I mention so much apparently can be broken when the family decides to move their loved ones to a nursing home: truth is that if the institution personnel has the capacity, knowledge, experience, and especially the vocation, they will help your loved ones find real sense of belonging in the institution, and they will also provide a happy life to you and a great comfort and wellbeing to the rest of your family, without the tough responsibility of taking care of them and taking decisions where plenty of your brothers might not agree with you. On this matter, DO NOT decide to take your loved ones to a nursing home without having talked about it with the rest of the family, and having reached an agreement.

Bear in mind that delegating the attention of your elderly loved ones to the institution or nursing home you analyzed, qualified, and picked is *an act of love*: definitively an act of loved towards them, towards you and towards the unity of the family. *Family unity* does not imply living altogether in the same place: it means that everyone is looking towards the same direction without forgetting that family is unity and love, regardless of how far geographically you might be from each other.

Now... you, who has the age and health circumstances that might need care around the clock, don't you think it's fair to prepare, start a "piggy bank" and use it to live the rest of your life in a place where you receive what you deserve? For this very reason I speak about the sense of belonging, especially when that place you feel you belong to is your decision, and not your sons' or grandsons'.

Don't leave to them the tough choice of what to do with your life when you face the situation of depending. This is a tremendous lack of responsibility. They have their lives and you don't have the right to alter them only because you did not establish it at the appropriate time.

IDENTITY

Another one of the points that are needed for the wellbeing of any human being is knowing what the reason of his existence in this planet is. I know that very often you have wondered what the mission or purpose of your presence in the world is; of course I understand that every day we have to get up, spruce up, get dressed, maybe take the kids to school and then off to work, but... do you really call *work* what you do to obtain money and manage to achieve your family's wellbeing? Are you like those who say: "pfff! Is it Monday again? Or, "thank God it's Friday!"? Or put in other words, do you think that your job is a "necessary evil" to achieve a comfortable financial status and an equally satisfactory life?

I have some more questions: Do you know what you want in your life? Do you know your true vocation?... When you look at yourself in the mirror, do you wonder if you are satisfied with who you are or with what you do? Do you know what your life mission is?

Some years ago, when I was hosting a radio show called "Kilometers of Life" (title suggested by my dear Grissell Vazquez, then director of the Radio Mujer radio station in Guadalajara, Jalisco), I had the opportunity to interview Facundo Cabral. He had problems with his flight and was not able to make it to the show, however, he sent one of his representatives, who offered an apology on Facundo's behalf, and told me that I was invited to his office in Guadalajara, in Chapalita neighborhood; I gladly accepted and I got to know a great human being: we spent several hours talking about my passion to sow the image of a dignified old age in Mexico and the experiences he had had in his life, his losses and the way he had managed to overcome his adversities. After two bottles of an Argentinian red wine and a Chilean one (which made me laugh, as he particularly enjoyed this last one) we came to several conclusions, among which I share this one: *"he who works or dedicates to something he does not enjoy is unemployed".*

This is the moment I tell you that comes in the life of many, of course, when old age is reached, when you ask yourself: "who am I"? "What am I here for?" "What am I good for?" "What good have I done in my life?" "Why am I still alive?"

This is called *identity*.

The old aged lacks from identity and this is caused due to living within a culture where chronologically "young" or physical beauty is established as prototype of health, where the obese individual, the elder, or the "disabled" is seen as someone that should not belong to the "normal" society.

I do not forget that stupid television ad where a young couple, in love with each other, is painting their apartment, and in the meantime, an old aged in a wheelchair was around, just looking; afterwards, one of them paints over the Martian too! With this action, the old man is presented as a piece of furniture in their apartment! And, do you know what the worst part is? That the old guy considers himself equally "invisible"!

I could keep on cursing about that ad I can't even remember what it was showing. What is very clear to me is that everything that surrounds the elderly makes you feel that his presence can become obsolete, useless, undesirable, and even disgusting!

The elder loses his *identity*. Most of the time he does not know his purpose in this life when he gets to this stage of life. He does not know the value of his presence, and of course this takes him to feeling obsolete, useless, undesirable, and dirty! What is next? Illnesses, every kind of malaise, depression, isolation, feelings of loneliness, of *invisibility*, and therefore –I insist– he becomes sick very easily!

When attending patients, I have observed an unpleasant position in most of the cases I mentioned before: the son takes the elder father or mother to consultation with things such as:

- "My father doesn't eat".
- "My mother doesn't sleep well".

And it is the son or daughter that speaks! The old aged has lost or left aside his preferences because most of the members of the *family thinks* he should not eat this or that! Furthermore, the doctor, besides of giving him a huge list of medications to "heal" the ailments his sons are complaining about, gives him another list full of restrictions both in his food and in his emotions. And, you know what the most logical thing for the elder to think is? ... "Then, what is the point of living if I am not even allowed to enjoy exciting experiences?".

The grandfather or the elderly loses his *identity*.

... as *consequence*, he defines and accepts that he is sick, or that he is a clinical case and that whatever life is left for him to live is not up to him, but to those who "take care" of him: he accepts that there is NOTHING left to do.

One of the elements that are contained in the "formula" I have reflected on for several years is *compassion*. The application of this formula would heal each and every one of the ailments in the world if it was applied. It is the GAWFFALC [1] formula.

Compassion IS NOT pity: it is putting yourself in someone else's shoes, perceiving the happenings of the daily life from his point of view, *living* those significant moments in which he again feels as a member of a family, productive, loved, participating and interactive, both in society as in his surroundings, especially his family.

I strongly suggest that you put yourself in the shoes of your family's old aged, and if there are not, in those of any elder you know.... What do you feel? Ok! In the shoes of any old stinky

---

[1] This "formula", GAWFFALC, means: Gratitude, Acceptance, Work, Faith, Forgiveness, Attitude, Love, Compassion. It will be explained with detail later on.

beggar that asks you for "a little help, for the love of God"! Do you think he is asking for a coin because he only has the need for money? Yes, of course! But his greatest need is feeling *significant* in the lives of those who surround him again! They would rather receive a smile than a coin, as the smile pulls them closer to life, as well as to *validity and <u>identity!</u>* The coin you could give to him puts them closer to dependency and to... providing for his lazy sons!

For a moment, close your eyes and feel, perceive, place yourself inside the feelings of the elder of your family... do you feel him happy? Full? Loved? Satisfied for what he has achieved in his life and in his family? INDEPENDENT? If so, congratulations, as I think you are one of those rare cases where this exists. But otherwise, it is time to start thinking in what you would do and how you would feel when you get to that age and start preparing yourself in every sense.

"The human being was born to transcend and not to depend".

<u>It is not possible to transcend without identity or with a *valid* personal history.</u>

Deal with the *need of identity* of your aged loved ones in the present moment and you will be sowing the presence of identity in your future, as it is YOUR responsibility.

Identity is being oneself. It is not allowing someone to criticize the way you dress, the way you are, eat or have fun; it is overcoming to plenty of those habits and customs that have been with us for many decades, in which the elder ladies have to wear black dresses with white polka dots, from the neck to the floor, not curse, not show their feelings, be submissive or quiet, accepting all the customs (I completely agree with Ricardo Arjona when he says that the worst thing ever is to carry on with the customs and habits); identity is daring to break all of those burdens and daring to be oneself, at 60 or 100 years old, not giving a damn about the comments (envies) of any other person.

Ha! It is curious to recognize that the one criticizing you is in fact an admirer, someone who envies you, because he has not dared as you have.

Identity is life, value, presence, validity, visibility... it is love, love for oneself. Loving oneself is a basic rule to have identity and transcendence. And, do you know what is also very important in this regard? The fact that you always keep your identity! You will be an example! The best legacy to your sons and grandsons!

Identity cannot be buried: it is perennial, but you need to fight to keep it valid! Remember: it is YOUR responsibility!

GOALS

There is a beautiful Buddhist-Tibetan blessing that is used when the moment to say goodbye presents. It says:

"May God bless you and grant you EVERYTHING you wish and desire, but ONE thing".

Of course, in that moment, you wonder what that thing is, and of course, that same question is made to the one offering it. The answer is: any one thing or any one goal, since, as long as you fight to obtain it or to achieve it, you will be happier: you will have something to live for.

Certainly, when you are part of a family and a society, the needs for education arise, and afterwards, practice your major once you have earned your degree; you rent and equip your office, you hire the staff you think you are going to need, and you start by advertising your services, etc., only that, as always, the question appears in my head: is that the profession the one you consider appropriate for you?

I know plenty, plenty of people that once the hangover from the graduation party has passed, they perceive the sensation of "¿what's next?". "What do I do, now that my student life is over?" As luck may have it, I have run into some of these people after many years and I ask them how they did in their professional life (most of my classmates are already retired) and their response is a simple "- okay. I am already retired and I don't know what to do". Others say: "- late did I realize that medicine was not my vocation. However, since it was the only thing I knew, I kept on going up to this moment and I still don't know what I'm good for... if I'm good for anything" ... I hear the following remarks so many times: "thank God it's Friday!", or: "pfff... Monday again!". I bring back to the table what Facundo Cabral and I were talking about the afternoon of a very luminous day which I already spoke about in previous lines:

"he who dedicates to something he does not enjoy or does not like is unemployed".

I ask you up front: what you do in this moment of your life makes you happy? Do you enjoy it? Or, on the contrary, do you consider it to be a need for the sustenance of your life? Please think before answering: visualize yourself every morning after getting up... do you do it smiling of joy because you consider it a new opportunity to grow up and fulfill your dreams? Chase your goals? Creating? Innovating? Setting your ambitions and *goals* straight?

Personally, the word *"work"* should not be understood as:

"The activity you need to do as an obligation to obtain a payment in return".

But:

"Work is the activity that, when done, allows us to express our vocation, what we love, and that, <u>in addition </u>we receive an economic retribution".

Human being is... no... not only the human being, but every living being that has goals –besides other factors that I will mention later on... happy! Everything, absolutely everything that lives and even those things that is not alive has a purpose or goal in life! The flower is happy just by being it even though it may live only for a few hours! If we could understand the language of a butterfly we would know how happy it is every instant of its life!

What is the dream you long the most? And if you do not have one, why don't you have one?

And if you do have it, why not establish another wish, another goal to accomplish, another creation, another summit to conquer?

This work is not one for personal development; it does not give you advise to lose weight, or to improve your sex life, or anything like it, but plenty, plenty more: it tries to help you make your life a work of art, so that when you contemplate it at any given moment, even in death, you feel proud, to the point of maybe shedding a tear of pride and satisfaction, until it stops in your smile!

At this moment, and with the excitement that causes in me imagining you having an expression of intensity and –I deeply wish for this– motivation, this question comes to mind: What is a goal?... Is it ok in a book of this nature to leave this as homework for the reader? Yes, it is ok! Personally, a goal is something that gives you a reason to live, to work your butt off to achieve it, in chasing it and chasing it despite the negative remarks you may hear, which are filled with envy; a goal, or chasing a dream is something that may cause insomnia, and that in the dark of your room in the night, makes you smile when looking at you in the process, in the journey, and all this without harming anyone or anything... a goal, or chasing a dream places us in the category of creators, innovators, breakers of paradigms and habits, customs which real name is burden, obstacle, trap and despondency.

*"Dream big... dream VERY big; aim high... aim VERY high, and when you hear comments and criticisms that contain things such as: it's impossible, he's crazy, he won't make it, it is because you are in **the right track***".

Also bear in mind that the negative comments that others emit only contain expressions of envy.

And remember that *"every flatterer is a hidden enemy"*. (I stole this phrase from my buddy Solon).

Something that I find "funny" is that when you go to great lengths and you even pawn your soul to accomplish that thing you believe in, and does not "satisfy" or is not "approved" by the rest of the people, you are called stubborn, senseless, crazy and even idiot, but when you manage to make that dream come true and reach the desired goal, the same people that criticized you immediately call you tenacious, persistent, fighter, winner, etc. Funny, isn't it?

I will seize this moment to recognize Nicola Tesla, the real genius, and also noble, who chased his dreams, and made them come true. Others stole them from him... Undoubtedly, when one wants to act with a noble heart, others take advantage of this beautiful characteristic, use it for their benefit, and call us "idiots". Isn't that right, sergio? (Lower case). (He knows what I'm talking about).

Thus, we define that as long as you have goals and autonomy or liberty (another one of the points we will talk about later), you will be happy, since:

"It is preferable to die trying, looking to accomplish a goal, than getting to the moment of your death and being sorry for not having at least tried".

Goals are these and even others, from the affective, spiritual, material kind, writing a book, seducing the neighbor... etc.

Therefore, when we stop being us, we abandon most of our dreams or goals, and we follow those that have been established by the rest of the people: we live to please what has been established by them.

Now, I want to make the difference between goals and competition very clear. Real *goals* are our own; the *competition* is the eagerness to be, achieve or possess more than the neighbor, the brother, somebody else, since the goals are personal, individual, our own. Surely you could get a better car than John Doe, a 100 inch curve screen or travel in your own jet, but the real goals, the real dreams are those that make us feel like a better human being, and in most of the cases we don't notice them, until it is a little too late, just as the case of a patient I had some years ago: a dying millionaire whose only wish was to tell his late wife that he loved her, as he never did so while she lived; I helped him visualize her and even encouraged him to say it out loud, which he did while crying and filled with emotions. He died two days later.

Don Armando possessed a huge fortune. He was gravely ill, and at the end of his life, his greatest wish was to have a cognac snifter, while the stupid doctor attending him had forbidden it and the… relatives followed his scientific instructions until Don Armando died… died with the craving of having a last zip of cognac: *the most expensive thing in the face of earth is that which you cannot even get with money.*

Chase your goals, dream big and fight with teeth and nails to make them come true, and don't mind them being materials, as the material possessions let us know what we are capable of, but don't confuse them with the competition"

In many moments of my life, when being close to people in their terminal stage, I have asked them what their greatest desire in that precise moment is, and you wouldn't guess the variety of things I have heard. This is why I confirm that there IS such a thing as "what if", because when we are close to our final moment, plenty of things cross our mind. Rumor has it that when you go through a near-death experience, especially in some sort of accident, you see in front of your eyes a series of images, just as if it was a movie; I do not agree with this. I know that you see in front of your eyes everything you have not done, every "I forgive you" you did not give or receive, every situation that shares the "what if" and the fear of dying without having done it saddens you.

A very powerful goal is to forgive. Consider this: it will set you free!

Therefore, don't leave for tomorrow what you can do today: don't allow yourself to go to bed without saying "I love you" to that person you love; don't hesitate in forgiving or apologizing when you understand that you have hurt someone… don't go to bed without planning what you will be doing next day... next week... the rest of your life, and most of all, don't forget to *thank* whoever is the object of your beliefs for the privilege of having one more day to fulfill your aspirations, to chase your dreams and keep on dreaming... planning.

You should not worry if you don't achieve your goals, since worrying is a loss of time. Take a break, review the processes you have applied to make that dream come true, and think if you maybe have to use another approach, as there is no plan B, but route B or C, probably D... but, never give up!

Bear this in mind:

"Wanting is believing, believing is creating, creating is growing and making the people that surround you grow".

Also, remember that:

"A butterfly is just a worm with experience".

MATERIAL POSSESSIONS

Knowing that you are the owner of a real estate property, of an apartment in front of the beach or a cabin in the woods, of a car as luxurious as you wish, of a very special watch, the satisfactory process of going shopping and acquiring the clothes that make you feel fancy and comfortable without looking at the price tag, of going to the trendiest restaurant, and ordering what catches your eye and looks the tastier, without looking at the list at the right of the menu are of course satisfactions, and is another one of the elements that the human being requires to feel good with himself, in his work and in his familiar and social groups!

Do you remember how it feels when you are opening the box that contains what you had desired for so long, and you scrutinize it, you look at it again and again, without noticing the huge smile your face is showing? The way a new car smells when leaving the dealership? What does it feel like? Am I making you reminisce? Well, enjoy it again! Surely this already forms part of one of your goals, which fills you with immense satisfaction, as it represents the result of your efforts to obtain something that is *yours*: it is the *prize* to your work and your tenacity and faith in yourself. Oh! Did you buy that dress that during plenty of weeks or months you saw in the store window and you imagined yourself wearing it and receiving the looks of men and women while walking down the street? How satisfied are you?

Now, the opposite: you buy inexpensive, or second hand clothes, since your financial resources are limited, you travel by bus, you understand that what you are paid in your job is not what you deserve, however, you don't argue or do anything to improve, since you consider that it is better to have something in your hand than promises of businesses or wages that never come; you quit to the possibility of going to some restaurant because "it is only for rich people", or even worse, when you accept that phrase, falsely attributed to Jesus, that says: "if you ambition for something more than what you have or what you get to eat, dress and live, it is a sin!!"...

In a very personal point of view, as I have lived infinity of financial contrasts during my life, I tell you that "poverty does not exist, but the attitude of being poor (financially speaking) does". Adopt Mike Todd's phrase; it says: "I have never been poor. I have only been without money. Being poor is a mental state and not having any money is a temporary condition". In the same measure you underestimate your ability to achieve the benefits that brings the financial wealth, you will be and will financially live a mediocre situation. I have in my memory those movies with Pedro Infante, Sara Garcia, Chachita and Prudencia Grifell, where misery was a common factor, and where the actors of all of those movies left a mark that was hardly erased, where the Mexican is (has to be) poor; where he begs to God for money all day, constantly drunk, crying and suffering (enjoying... comfort zone) his poverty and misery, emphasizing that those who have money and power are "evil". They even accept humiliations from rich people... tears, drama, scarcity, limitations, cigarettes accompanying those moments and, you know what? We took it for granted, and we even admired every character those actors interpreted! The "terrible truth" was that all of them lived VERY good, financially speaking, as even Pedro Infante died in his own plane! He was not an alcoholic! Meanwhile, plenty of Mexicans accepted the idea that being poor and living in poverty is a way to reach the "heavens".

Being financially rich is not a "sin", and neither is it "bad"; love for the neighbor starts in the love for ourselves, and we cannot help, drive or motivate no one if we don't start with ourselves, and it is absolutely undeniable that possessing financial means allows us to provide help.

In many of my conferences, I ask the auditorium to share who the 3-5 most important people in their life are, and most of them say things such as: "my children, my mother, my father, my husband...", and I then ask them, where are you? If you take the food out of your mouth to feed the hungry you will starve to death and the "hungry" will keep on living, manipulating and begging!

Calm down... calm down... Having, possessing is wonderful, but, be careful! Never allow the things you have acquired to steer your life. Never allow yourself to feed your "possession". I invite you to read Victor Hugo's profound poem, called "I Wish", where he comments very accurately that there comes a time where you need to put yourself in front of your possessions and let them know that it is you who possess them, and not the other way around, since living to support them will ruin your life and the lives of those who surround you and who you claim to love.

Show off and enjoy all the things you get with your work, or better said, with the expression of your vocation, doing what you love and what you were born to do; perceive the delicious scent of that perfume you just bought, enjoy the vacations you bought after a year's work, of squeezing your brain, your abilities, and above all, your vocation, but something very important: never allow something or someone to establish a way of life for you; sharpen your senses, the world is filled with cons, jealousies and lies, and people that take advantage of your good intentions and your love, and then consider you an idiot! And then go on and build their world and their material wealth based on what you have given them.

You are so much more than you can imagine! You were not born to beg! You were not born to be mediocre, or a character of those soap operas where having limitations makes you the "hero". *Decree* being financially rich, envision yourself driving the car of your choice and dreams, enjoying the most delicious feasts you have only seen in movies... EVERYTHING that you see and you consider "out of your reach" was considered just the same by their current owners. Personally, I admire Sylvester Stallone for having achieved his series of movies "Rocky" when his financial resources were close to zero, as well as

J.K. Rowling with her "Harry Potter" series... the real poverty –I insist— is, resides in the one you accept and decide to live; therefore, why not choose to be financially rich?

I repeat Mike Todd's phrase: "I have never been poor. I have only been without money. Being poor is a mental state and not having any money is a temporary condition".

We have to live based on *decisions* and not on *consequences*.

The decisions are taken by you; the consequences are product of the decisions of many others, of many customs and habits that are mostly filled with burdens.

The present point is represented by the *material possessions* and the importance they have in your everyday life and in your whole life.

As much as you feel satisfied of desiring, pursuing and accomplishing being owner of that what makes you feel happy, forms part of the 12 elemental points for you to feel good with yourself (the top priority) and with the rest of the people.

Go and obtain that material object that will make you feel good. Pay for it up front. And enjoy it right away to the full while you are alive, as you will not take it with you when you die.

Happy material achievements!

Now, the painful reality: especially in our Mexican culture, it is *established* –and we accept it— that we need to make a great effort, work until our strengths and desires to pursue our dream have been depleted; achieve a financial wellbeing to immediately pass it on! You know that I don't hold back my expressions or words when I say this: That sucks! Work so that others enjoy our financial achievements? So that they don't go through the same limitations and scarcities we did during aaall of our life? NOT A CHANCE! They should get to work! Let our kids and grandkids build based on *their own efforts* the wellbeing they deserve! Yes, let's help them in their times of need and crises, but let's NOT solve the problem for them, because, as long we do that, we will create co-dependencies, guilt feelings, obligation feelings, misunderstood responsibilities and that may lead us to very uncomfortable situations among our sons, grandsons and us. And what is worse: family ruptures, disputes among brothers, distancing, resentments, stupid legal procedures with the objective of establishing "equality and justice" when trying to distribute the material possessions you left.

Establish limits to help without *expecting to get paid*, but limit that help; while you do that, enjoy your achievements and keep this phrase in mind, which I use as title of a conference I have travelled the country giving:

"If you don't fly first class, your inheritors will".

It is so common to see that the grandpas are visited very frequently by their relatives when they are alive and wealthy, but as soon as a will or an in-life inheritance is established, they gradually stop getting those visitors.

Some years ago, a dear friend of mine had prostate cancer and his medical diagnosis was negative in the short term due to the metastasis to the bone that was already present, so he decided to distribute his possessions while still alive. Up to that moment, we received the visit of his sons every day, who took turns to visit him during the morning and during the afternoon; during the night, he had a nurse, whose attention was excellent.

The day came when he signed his will before the notary, where he described who would receive each one of his properties, money, big positions in companies, etc. 6 weeks after that moment, the visits of his sons (to be understood as "inheritors") started spacing out, until they showed up only once or twice a month for a brief moment. No more taking him out to a restaurant or to any kind of celebrations.

He fell into a profound deception, and of course, he fell into a depression, so deep that he sometimes cried with me, expressing the pain that discovering the real love his sons "felt for him" caused him. This caused me indignation and started to plan something... on his birthday, I called up his sons and daughters and organized a barbeque with beers, sauces, chorizo, pearl onions and something he enjoyed very much: rum –or "roncito", as he called it—. And yes, everyone attended, some sharp and some late, but the point is that in the middle of the celebrations, after the traditional "happy birthday", blowing up the candles and cutting the cake, I waited for the precise moment and told my friend in a voice loud enough for everyone to listen, but soft enough so that it seemed like a question only directed to him:

– "Hey... and where do you keep the centenarios[2] you showed me that day when we were talking about your memories and your life? There were quite a bunch, right?".

He, for a fraction of a second, was surprised, but managed to recompose his facial expression when understanding the sense and content of my question, and immediately showed a question in his face, and rubbing his chin, kept on trying to remember where that supposed collection of centenarios was.

Magical moment.

Everyone left their glasses and beers and then –not without sharing looks between each other— asked him:

– "You have centenarios, daddy?".

One of the daughters said:

– "Daddy, that was a well-kept secret!".

---

[2] The "Centenarios" is a Mexican gold bullion coin with a value of $50 pesos, that were first minted in 1921 to celebrate the first centenary of the Mexican Independence; their fabrication was suspended in 1931 and afterwards it was resumed in 1943; given the demand for the golden coins of 0.900 purity. They were not coined again.

Obviously, yes, obviously, he responded that he had some, but that he could not remember where he had put them, as so much time has passed by and could not bring it to his mind. He concluded that as soon as he found them he would let them know, as there was a fair amount.

And, guess what? The visits of the "loving sons" once again became frequent!

Weeks later, between "roncito and roncito", we were guffawing because of that scene we had played. One day, he hugged me for a big period of time and said:

– "You son of a gun! I don't only consider you my friend, but also my son… Thanks for everything!". Then he kissed my cheek while a tear ran down his face. Darn it… another one ran down mine too!

He died a few weeks later, I went to his funeral and in it, one of his sons asked me if I knew where those darned centenarios were… I could not tell him the truth, and my response was a "no, I don't know".

SOCIALIZATION

The illness I most commonly find in the old aged is *the loneliness*. Isolation leads to loneliness, which leads to depression, and depression is the proper condition for any other ailment to be installed and surely end up requiring medical attention, medicines, and other elements that will set and label the elder as an "ill person".

I clearly understand that our current culture *fears* the old age and through every means it is established that most of the happiness resides in moments with friends –especially chronologically young— with wines, cigarettes, sex and even drugs of every kind, and the get-togethers of the old aged are not seen in the same way, and are even a reason to make jokes on, such as "The Dead Bird club", and "The Jurassic Park", among many more.

As we live more years, we realize that our youth friends start dying one by one, and this affects us terribly, as one becomes aware of the closeness of death, suffering, dependencies, and of course, significant deterioration of our quality and dignity of life.

Accepting that living many years is "aging" and that consequently we have to accept also what most of the elder live: loneliness, diseases, limitations, dependencies, invisibility, absence in their family and social groups, leads them to live old… to half live or live dead and wait that others decide for them until their final moment.

However, when an elder, whatever his age may be, revolts against the mentioned concepts and continues to go out with his lifelong friends, laughing at their current situations, playing cards, chess, checkers and even designating a day of the week to have coffee and enjoying the activities of every person in the street, admiring the female beauty while doing so, or masculinity in the case of the ladies, planning trips, dances, celebrations, birthdays and celebrating life without letting the "ailments that come with the age" get in the way, these individuals will be *socializing*, or crossing out another one of the needed points I have mentioned, and will be setting the bricks for a real home where a happy and full old age can be lived.

Among the activities I have done in geriatric centers, nursing homes or, old people's homes! (let's not waste time with euphemisms, it's the same anyway, and IN NO WAY these places resemble those gloomy places we were shown in the past), has been taking a van with plenty of seats and taking them for a ride, having a beer, some chicharron or carnitas tacos and just sit down to check out the ladies or the guys that are passing by; this –I assure it— is living! And thus, I notice how they change their expressions when a girl with spectacular breasts or a guy with spectacular butt passes by! You should see the face in the old girls in that moment! That is socializing, living, what everyone else is living, without age or "moral" being important, or what has been established as "correct or incorrect", "good or bad", "normal or abnormal": enjoy the freedom of having "ocular orgasms"!

Getting together periodically grants great benefits, one of them, VERY important, is to know that one is mortal. Yes! Knowing that probably in the next reunion someone will not be there! This, despite not being spoken about by the members of the same group, establishes the sense of *acceptance* of one's own mortality, and of course, preparing for death itself.

But not everything is so tragic! Socializing is re-living, re-creating, being re-born, laughing, crying, longing for something, remembering... living! The individual that socializes goes to bed laughing of what was shared during the reunion, and therefore, that wellbeing is reflected in his health, in the releasing of the tension, in the increasing of the serotonin, the endorphins and dopamine, substances of happiness and hence, reduction of the unpleasant moments of the day, and maybe of the ailments he has to endure. Socializing is an elemental part of the living being, and especially for the human being.

I should emphasize that those moments are *necessary* to be listened to! It is a wonderful opportunity to speak without being criticized, speaking about our dreams without being minimized, showing off our achievements without them generating envies, talking about our sons and grandsons and of those few or plenty moments we live with them. Yes: *we live with them!* When getting back home, we will feel an extraordinary relief and it will be impossible going to bed with less pain and with a smile in our faces!

Now, something very, very important: organize get-togethers where you speak about life, maybe about the past or about the future plans, close or not, but please, PLEASE don't speak about the illnesses and the medicines you take! Don't speak about the doctors that see you or transmit what you read or heard! When I go to reunions of old aged people (what does being old aged means, please? 50 years old? 70? 100? 200?), I hear things such as: what do you take for your high cholesterol? Did you already take your PSA [3]? Hey, are you still doing the mammogram? Please, shut up with the crap already! Your life will be healthier in the same measure where you don't give value or power to the "diseases"; life is beautiful in every sense, as far as you consider your bumps and bruises as learning; nothing, NOTHING of what happens to you during your life lacks of a didactic value, but the sense you grant to what happens to you during it is YOUR responsibility, and you could say that your life is miserable because you lost your loved ones, or because you don't have any money, or because you have diabetes or cancer: life will always be more beautiful and with a bigger and deeper content if you understand that nothing happens by chance, and that everything you receive is learning, whatever it is! Your growth is not based on what life offers to you, but on what you do with it and this is experience, lear-

---

[3]   Prostate-Specific Antigen

ning... evolution! And I could even say *rebirth*!

Our lives are filled with *experiences*, but experiences ARE NOT what life gives you, *but what you do with them*.

Don't manipulate your reunions trying to stand out because of you "suffering". It is clear in my mind that generally we try to be or have *more* than the rest in any get-together: we try to stand out in anything, whether it is having the best watch, brand clothes and in many, many cases, standing out because of *suffering* greater ailments than those mentioned in the reunion. I have heard things like:

–"I was taken to the hospital two days ago with an u-n-b-e-a-r-a-b-l-e pain I had; I was examined all day and after plenty of studies I was told that I had a kidney stone that when passing through my body until it was out, causes a pain so big that can cause one to faint or sometimes even go into shock...".

Ah! But two chairs away is Maria Dolores, who immediately replies with:

– "That is not pain! Pain is what I felt when my poor baby got stuck and could not be born! They had to use forceps to get him out! Now, that is pain!

And so on... those reunions where no socialization happens take place. And more importantly, you don't fulfill the principal objective: having fun!

I can't stop from sharing what I lived with my dear friend Carlos Rangel when we were invited to the civil marriage of a very "nice" couple, and we didn't have any money to buy anything in their gift wish list (there was not going to be a religious wedding, so the gifts were supposed to be given that day), so we decided to go to Tequila, Jalisco, we bought a gallon of white tequila that was $175 pesos, yes, $175 pesos for a gallon! We mixed it with some cola-flavored drink so that it turned into a mature colored tequila, and we filled 4 handcrafted bottles with it. When tasting it, the father of the bride told us:

– "What an exquisite tequila! This is a cognac! Congratulations on your delicate taste when choosing this gift for my daughter!".

Weeeeell, (as my friend Claudia says), it was considered to be only for the "sybarite palates".

I can go on telling things I have listened to in plenty of occasions that could crack you up (sorry, they won't crack you... they will only make you laugh, maybe up until you lose control of your sphincter).

Socializing: extraordinary occasions that *have* to be organized with a set frequency to speak about the *poem* of life, of the *work of art* that we live on every moment and seizing the bumps and bruises that are given to us to learn and grow.

The afternoons or moments you spend with your pals have to leave you a very nice taste in your mouth: from preparing to attend to those reunions, using those clothes you only use in "special occasions" (socializing is a special occasion! So don't save up anything "special" for "special occasions": use your best perfume, your best dress, jacket, tie, etc., but most importantly, your best smile). When finishing the get-together, you should come back home with an immense satisfaction.

All the above sounds fantastic, but do nowadays elders practice this? Do they socialize as they require?

Think it through and you will notice that this one is yet *another* factor that most of our old aged lack of.

AFFECTIVITY

I think I have to share with you that after personal investigations related to why "it is not the same thing to get old in Spanish as it is in English" (that is the title of a book that made me understand several things regarding aging in many cultures and eras throughout their history), I found the 12 points I am putting in this work with plenty of enthusiasm, but most importantly with the desire of you making your old age a wonderful adventure; naturally, I have looked for ways to spread what I have learned through several means, and that is why I have written articles for various magazines nationally, newspapers, radio shows, sections in some TV shows, complete TV shows, conferences, workshops, congresses... well, several means with the same objective.

In the "Radio Mujer" radio station in Guadalajara, with my program "Kilometros de Vida", I also spread everything I considered important, chasing the objective I mentioned. I feel lucky because I received several calls from people congratulating me, asking for orientation, asking for medical or familiar consultation, and plenty, plenty more; one of those people was a 54-year-old woman who asked me for the opportunity to speak with me about her personal situation with her boyfriend and family.

We met in a coffee shop, and told me her name (Monica). She had widowed more than 7 years ago, and told me that recently, around 8 months ago, she had started going out with a man who asked her to have a formal relation with him and maybe get married. When they went out, they met in a spot in downtown Guadalajara, and he dropped her some blocks away from her home, since they did not want her kids to find out about this.

We spoke for quite a while, I congratulated her and encouraged her to keep on going with this relationship, and to seek keeping on living with a new illusion, and this made her feel like she was doing the right thing, as she had told me that her parents had told her that she had to "show respect to her late husband by not getting married or not having any relation whatsoever with any other man".

I won't bore you telling you everything I told her, the answers to her questions, until she asked me to go to her house and eat with her family and that she would take advantage of that moment to let everyone know that she was seeing someone, and that she would formalize her relation with him, maybe because she felt stronger.

I showed up the day and time we had agreed upon, she introduced me to her kids as the radio host of the shows were the personal development of the elders was spoken about (…). Everything was going ok, in spite of the fact that I could tell she was nervous, unsettled, looking at me as if she was trying to look for the courage to "confess" to their children her love for other man that was not their father.

Finally, she plucked up her courage, stood up and said:

– "Kids, I want to let you know that I have recently started going out with a friend who treats me wonderfully and has asked me to be his girlfriend for now, and if we get along, we'll see what comes up in the future. I want you to know it and that I don't want to harm the memory of your father, but also, I don't want to be alone when you start doing your lives".

The oldest son dropped his spoon with an abrupt movement, looked her to her eyes, while his face showed harshness, and almost spitting his words, he said:

– "Mom, at your age with that nonsense?".

Another one of her daughters, with face like a guanabana, stood up and almost shouting, told her off:

– "Mom, are you going to dishonor my father's memory with that nonsense?".

The oldest son just stood up and left the room without saying half a word, wearing a disappointment expression in his face... then he approached back to the table, grabbed his plate, still with food, took it to the kitchen's trash can and threw away its content, and then left his plate in the sink without much touch.

Monica's face dropped and she started crying.

I remind you that this work is not a Yolanda Vargas Dulche novel, so I won't tell you what followed that moment, as there is no case to it, but I want you to see the profound obtuse background of those attitudes we call habits or customs, and that is in no way culture, and that applies to age, widow status, and lack of exercise of the rights of those who need *love* to live!

Affectivity is a component needed by every human being. Love and being loved is *essential to* live with quality. Love is a huge motivator in every sense; when you are loved, you are more productive, there is no such thing as "depression", you sleep well, take advantage of the nutriments contained in your meals, your arterial pressure is closer to normal or is normalized, you give a comic touch to everything you go through, you perceive and irradiate wellbeing, you consider everything you see around as wonderful, worthy of being enjoyed, and this, all of the mentioned elements grants you happiness, health, LIFE! Without your age, the age difference, the financial or social situation being important... *"the limits of love are not attached to the conditions or chronological situations, but those of intensity"*. (Pepe Valencia).

The beautiful human being Mario Benedetti once said: *"We all need an accomplice; someone that helps us use the heart"*.

Now, I want to point out something very important when it comes to loving. The first person you need to love, feel affect, admire, is yourself. Otherwise, you will not be able to love someone else, or even something else, animal or thing. Every morning, look inside you, and before getting up from bed say out loud:

– "Today will be a wonderful day. I will feel loved and will love everything that surrounds me, especially myself".

Then, look at the mirror and don't mind the fact that you may have as many wrinkles as an unmade bed after a night of passion of a newly married couple, and say with absolute certainty:

– "I am handsome (or pretty) and sensual. What my face and body show is not but the passing of the wonderful experiences that I have decided to enjoy and that life has given me".

Then... off you go! Go and conquer your day... your whole day. At night, once you have come back to your home, take off your clothes, put on your pajama (if you use one, as sleeping naked is an exquisite experience... you should try it), and then thank yourself for having lived alive one day.

The point is, love without limits, establish what you want to enjoy regarding affectivity or love, define up to where you want to take any relation, regardless of what people may say, because, as I had already mentioned, those who criticize you are really expressing a hidden admiration for you.

One day, in one of the many, many shopping malls in Guadalajara, a couple of elders were kissing in the mouth, something that is not very frequent. The stupid comments of some of the passersby were: "yuck, gross!". "Look at them! So old and so horny!". Others spoke more with their gestures than their words. Now I ask you: At what age should one stop loving? Stop kissing? Hugging? Looking at your couple with heart shaped eyes, as my grandma Chicha used to say?

The old aged, or the grandfathers these days "must" –what an idiotic remark I just came up with, but it is real— hide their feelings, or be criticized by the members of their family and of the surrounding society. This is one more of the reasons they feel depressed for, since they have to renounce to this or at least hide.

Another one of my unforgettable patients (I already said I don't like the word, but I just use it so that we can understand each other better) was an 88-year-old man, who had as day nurse the most spectacular woman in the world –according to his appreciation—. She was 49 years-old, had widowed and had two sons. Every time I had the delicious opportunity of checking him, and above all, learn from him, and then leave a prescription for some medication that barely had an effect, he "confessed his love for his nurse". I congratulated him. He asked me if it would be "ridiculous" to propose marriage to her. I told him that it would be ridiculous not to!

It is better to be cynical than hypocritical.

The following week, I received a call from her, who asked me to meet somewhere outside Don Francisco's (my patient) house.

I attended with curiosity. We had barely sit down when she said that Don Francisco had asked her to marry him, or at least to move in with him. He was an elegant, educated man with excellent manners, and with enough money for the rest of his (or their) lives. He may not be a Sean Connery, but he had his charm and masculine expression.

I asked her about her thoughts on that, and her answer was that she had never considered it, but that he had asked her to sleep on it for a few days. That is why she called me. She insisted in asking me what she should respond to him. She certainly made me aware of her admiration for him and his attentions, and that "despite being old, he was good looking".

I should not leave aside two facts that are very real and concrete, and the word might not be "uninhibited", but more like cynical. Don Francisco was looking for company, someone to love and someone that loved him, in this case Marcela: that was her name. She, for her part, desired to be treated as a lady, being loved and of course, we can't leave aside her financial wellbeing!

I made her aware of the elements I mentioned, who humbly accepted. Immediately, I almost yelled:

– "The perfect combination! One has what the other one needs!" Although, Marcela", I said, "you don't know how much he is going to live and how he is going to live the above process, so maybe, just maybe, the best thing for you to do is to accept his proposal of living together and then making a definitive decision, since, given Don Francisco's age, it would be a definitive decision: *final!*".

They lived together for 2 months and got married right away. The criticisms emerged, but silently. They lived together for 2 and a half more years until he passed away, but had the opportunity to love and to say it out loud, and making every member of his family and his circle aware of this! But what I consider spectacular is that he had –they had— the courage of breaking those stupid paradigms that establish that love is only limited to young people. Their lives were completely different, he got better of his sicknesses and she enjoyed a financial wellbeing that she had not imagined. However, there is a "but": Marcela came to love him very much, really very much, and when he passed away, all she did in his funeral was praise the human quality and the love Don Francisco gave to her each one of the days they lived together.

I ask to you again: at what age *should* one stop loving? Should the stupid chronological limits be really respected to pursue love and affectivity? No freaking way! Love, chase your dreams, don't consider yourself a *weird* person only because there are feelings that boil inside you towards someone else who most certainly feels the same about you... and if you feel pointed or criticized, you can tell them to go fu... go fu... to go have fun at the nearest park! And follow your hunches. BE YOU and don't imitate or accept suggestions or criticisms based on envies. Definitely that will make you *live alive* until the last moment, when you *die alive*.

SEXUALITY

Ssssexuality! It jumps to everyone's eyes! And of course it does! What would be of every living being without sexuality? We may be able to love and love and love, but the act of love is *always* preceded by the sexual act: THERE IS NO such a thing as love at first sight; there is *attraction* at first sight, and then it goes on and on until that attraction finds a nice additive that over time becomes something beautiful: love.

The points I have described until now have truly been obtained over plenty of observation and comparisons with other cultures, other ages and, yes, with our culture from other times: Mayans, Aztecs, Otomi, Chichimecas, etc., and of course, from cultures from other countries; these observations have led me to think about how tremendously insignificant the image of the elder in current Mexico has fallen: do you know how many jokes there are regarding the "ailments" that those considered old suffer? You have surely listened to some or even have been victim of scathing remarks regarding age once you have passed the 40-year barrier… or even more so, after passing the 60-year barrier!

Some time after my separation from my first wife, when I was only 43 years old, I decided to invite a girl out who was around 22 years old (I guess), since I noticed her a little bit flirty every time I went to buy medicine for the residents of my nursing home "Albergue del Bosque". Her response was an immediate "yes, sure, I would be glad to!". My ego hypertrophied!

Just in time, she exited her working place, wearing a night dress, black, with an opening (it should be called "aperture", shouldn't it? Well, fashion stuff), she was marveled when I opened the car door for her, and also when I helped her with the chair at the restaurant we went to. The waiter had barely taken our order when she, with her eyes that showed a question mark, looking directly at my eyes, as if she was listening to my thoughts, and with a certain familiarity, asked me:

– "Doctor, why do you think I agreed to go out with you?"

My candid and innocent response was:

– "No... I don't know, you tell me".

– "Well, I wanted to know if men your age still like to make love...".

Freakin' immature brat! Then some more things I will not describe followed! I will just say that she called in sick the days that followed, and me, I spent some days with unforgettable pains in my hips, butt, legs and other parts of my anatomy.

Give me the chance to bluff...

You are aware that this contained a challenge, right? Well, I will not tell you what came after because it is not as relevant as what it made me understand: for the young, chronologically speaking, sex, desire and the immense satisfaction of the sexual act is simply inexistent for those who are older than 40!

My real and true quality of sexual life started after that age: 42 years. I understood that sex is poetry, but never hypocrisy; that the exercise of sexuality is extraordinarily delicious; that it is a very powerful motivation to pursue your goals; that as long as you don't lie and approach honestly and directly, without trying to hurt someone, you will find plenty of people that will respond "yes, let's do it" even though you may be proposing a strictly sexual encounter (sexuality and genitality is not the same): hugging and being hugged, kissing and being kissed, caressing and being caressed is something w-o-n-d-e-r-f-u-l! Let alone having sex (I wrote having sex and not making love... now imagine having sex with love! It is truly wonderful!).

Elementally, we are sexual beings from our birth. Sorry! We are born *precisely* because of a sex-genital act! This is: we are sexual beings before we are born, whether there is love or not, and we don't lose that sexuality until the moment of our death.

I can't forget Don Jesus, who at 99 years old, and at his home, he called me to have a glass of cognac and to tell me about how "hot" the nurses in his house during the day shift were, when they leaned over and showed what their cleavage could not hide, or when leaning facing the other way and showing their round behinds which made my teacher guffaw (I don't like the word "patient", so I have changed it for the word "teacher", but every now and then I say "patient"); I remember him with his skinny legs, swinging from his hospital bed in his house's main bedroom, talking to me about his past, his adventures, his girlfriends or lovers… I remember his tears rolling down his wrinkly face when he spoke to me about his love of the past. He said: "the love of my life" …

To justify my professional fees for the medical visit, I checked his blood pressure and I put the stethoscope against his chest while I looked at his face, and without really paying attention to what his heart was saying through its beats, I understood that the huge human being I had in front of me had managed to be what he was at that moment due to the security that having exerted his sexuality, represented even in that moment. Finally, I did establish a medical diagnostic, as I adopted my position as doctor.

At the current time of my life, I have understood that there are people that die more frequently because they have abstained from being themselves –sexually speaking– that those that stick to social or moral norms (–correction– pseudo-moral). Within the things I do with my terminally ill (also my teachers), is asking what is what they would most want to do in that moment of their lives. Of course, I have already spoken to them regarding the closeness to their death and I have received answers such as the case of a woman that had been director and owner of a big company in Guadalajara:

– "I would have liked to get myself a lover! What I lived with my husband was not what I considered worthy of my desires!".

I quote another teacher:

– "All I want in this moment of my life is a kiss from you, even if I die right away..!".

Don't think I feel like an Adonis because of this, nor my ego took off to the sky. I simply comment what I have heard trying to make myself clear about the fact that dying without fulfilling a dream is more painful that dying with all your illusions –of any kind– fulfilled.

I have heard many, believe me, many comments during these 40 years –up to now, year 2017– from tenths and tenths of human beings with plenty of needs, all of them from the sexual nature.

I should not leave aside the convictions I have acquired, thanks to their teachings, related to religion, its restrictions, concepts regarding "sin", "heaven" and "hell", "purgatory". And I mention this as a huge obstacle that has hindered them in being simply them.

There is a saying in Mexico: "youth, divine treasure" ... No, I do not agree. What are their foundations when they say this? Is it maybe having joints that are 100% functional? Instant erections? Immediate physiologic-sexual awakenings when seeing a naked man or a woman? Running 100 meters in 10 seconds? What if I told you that the old aged DOES NOT practice the sexual act in a gymnastic fashion, or breaking a record, maybe personal, or those that are established by a group of young men trying to outdo others? An elder, when practicing the sexual act, does it with rhythm, closing his eyes, waiting for a sigh or a gasp of his partner; he does it with patience and acceptance; gets close and kisses, gets close and caresses, gets close and feels, makes feel, even when there is no penetration or strict *genitality*.

There IS NO such thing as love at first sight: there is *attraction* at first sight and the attraction contains *sexuality*, not love: love is prudent and seeks us once it finds a smile in our faces, once we have exerted our sexuality, and I insist, not necessarily our genitality.

I gladly share what a woman said to me: she owned a very profitable company, and always walked with grace, elegance, distinction; her look was kindly defiant and considering her age, she had a very nice body. She had already widowed twice, without a known relationship at that moment. We became good friends, and in a burst of confidence, when I asked her what she regretted in his life, she leaned back in her chair, cleared her throat, took a zip of whisky and with her eyes lost in the horizon, replied:

– "Pepe… some years ago, I lived in a very big house, with an equally huge garden, which maintenance required the constant assistance of a gardener… (She made a pause, took a deep breath, smiled melancholically and continued): he was a biiiig man, with huge hands, always filled with callus and dirt; he had shoulders like a giant, and beautiful eyes. The features of his face were rough and he had very deep wrinkles. He was always sweaty, and that was not very pleasant to my nose. However, we both felt a very strong attraction. Naturally, I did not allow anyone –especially him– to suspect it, but I know that we both knew; I think my driver also sensed it but he played dumb.

She kept on seeing without watching while a roguish smile lighted up her face. I invited her to keep on speaking, and to tell me what caused her regret at that time, since she had already spoken so descriptively and eloquently about her gardener. She continued:

– "Well, my husband –second one, that is– elegant, always wearing a tie, with an impeccable suite and smelling like French perfume. He always spoke and ate properly, he had every attention with me, but did not ever touch me! And he did not excite me as the freaking gardener!

While saying the above, she slapped her leg with the palm of her hand, emphasizing her words. I laughed heavily and showed her my interest in keeping on listening.

– "Every time the gardener passed beside me, I felt shivers all over my body! I took my powder compact to review my makeup but what I really did was watching him through the mirror: I looked at his back, his butt, and you can imagine the rest of the things I felt.

All my interest was for her at that moment. I urged her to carry on. She almost screamed what followed:

– "What I regret today and for the remaining days of my life is not making him my lover! (She said this with other words). I imagined him caressing my whole body with his huge hands and doing everything my imagination and his were able to contain back then!!!

Do you really think that us elders don't have wishes, wet dreams, intense intentions of spending hours with a woman or a man (in my case, with a woman... and with respect to my wife, with plenty of women!)? Of course! Dozens of women wish –whatever their age may be– to have a "sexual party" with brawny men, or even with Afro-Americans guys with those special attributes that have been widely spread throughout the internet, and in any of these cases is this related to love! Only S-E-X!

Phew! That last paragraph was intense. But it is just the truth. You may be in denial, but even if you are, it will be inside you for the rest of your life.

Given the above, I feel a TERRIBLE DISCOMFORT: What happens with our actual elders that limit themselves to watching and imagining, knowing that if they express it, they will be victims of the stupid criticism (envy) of other people who have never considered that they will also become old, and that their feelings, especially sexuality and affectivity will remain.

Another one of the reasons why plenty of old aged currently live depressed is precisely because they feel "invisible" in this other factor. Instead of giving them anti-depressants, they should be pushed closer to life and to what marvelously exists in it: sunsets, sunrises, lips to kiss and lips that kiss us, human beings to love and human beings that love us, and this without letting the time factor affect us, since an hour of love and sexuality will make a huge difference in our lives.

I invite you to tell everyone to take a hike! Even if they are sons, grandsons, doctors, relatives, acquaintances, neighbors or whoever the hell might be trying to limit your ability to give and receive, to enjoy at any age the exquisite things of living… the delight… the blessing of the sexual expression.

I will take advantage of the moment and talk a little bit about erectile disfunction and testosterone.

Certainly, the levels of the production of this hormone, which is determinant for the desire and for the sexual function, starts to decrease over time, until we belong to the "Dead Birds Society". When you go to the doctor, what he prescribes the most is Viagra, Cialis or Levitra, since they fear that if they prescribe testosterone propionate, it could cause cancer. It is true that if your PSA (prostate-specific antigen) is high, you should not receive that medicine, as it would deteriorate that situation. What you should do is go to the doctor so that he can request the lab to determine your free and total testosterone. If they are low, you could receive those injections (testosterone propionate) without any problem. Testosterone DOES NOT cause prostate cancer: estrogens do (men also have estrogens), when being converted in estriol and estradiol due to the action of an enzyme that is called aromatase. There are medicines that inhibit the action of this enzyme and therefore you will be able to maintain relatively normal levels of your testosterone. Turn to your urologist for help and then, enjoy life!

I must also tell you that Viagra, Levitra, Cialis and other similar medicines DO NOT affect or damage your heart, no! The only existing counterindication is if you are taking medications that contain nitrites or Isosorbides. So, let me encourage you again to plan a night of crazy pleasure, but just be careful with the neighbors! If they hear you, they will think that you are having an insanity episode or something worse!

Oh! And something very important: if you die during your sexual act... well... VERY GOOD! You will die happy! Won't you?

SPIRITUALITY

I will always state that:

"We are spiritual beings living a human, earthly experience."

Given the above, I state that spirituality is inherent to every inhabitant of this Universe. Spirituality has nothing to do with religion. Moreover: religion obstructs; spirituality liberates: it makes you know what your mission in this Planet is; religion creates fears, spirituality grants peace and faith.

It is said that there are agnostic people (those who, without denying the existence of God, consider the notion of the absolute inaccessible to the human understanding) or the atheist, who does not believe in the existence of God. Well, I only want to know what would somebody that calls himself an atheist say when his car stops on the train tracks, and he suddenly hears its whistle, and the noise revealing that it is approaching at full speed? I am absolutely convinced that he would implore to any divine entity for him to be saved from being squashed. I don't think that there are atheists. I think that the concept of agnosticism is more congruent and honest than atheism, but that is not the subject I pretend to share with you.

Another of the elements that are needed for the human being to be considered in balance with himself and with his surrounding world is *spirituality*.

This does not mean attending daily or as frequently as someone from the past established as requirement to be a good adept to the religion he was born in or that he claims to practice.

I also do not accept that spirituality should mean not thinking in oneself, putting the obligation of satisfying the needs of others before one's needs, regardless of them being members of the family or not, including beggars, who take out of this a huge profit, asking for "a coin, for the love of God".

In my early childhood, every Sunday I attended to the 8am

mass with all of my brothers and my father, as this was the children's mass (...), and it was celebrated in Latin (I did not understand squat, I'll say it!); he woke us all up –we were 11 brothers and sisters... yes, eleven–, and with the exception of the youngest, we all attended mass. And yes, I was born inside the Christian Catholic religion, without knowing with certainty what I prayed, what I heard, and especially, the concepts of "sin", "hell", "limbo", "purgatory", what is considered "bad" and "good"; I listened that if you took your food out of your mouth (figuratively) and you gave it to your children, you would be rewarded by God. Likewise, stopping yourself from enjoying something that you craved could elevate you more and more until almost reaching the height or the position of a "saint"; I considered it horrible to think that if I touched my genitals, if I looked at the calves of a lady (I honestly didn't know at that time why every man did that), I was committing a "deadly sin", and I had to confess it to the priest, which most of the time fell asleep before me finishing my huge list of "sins". Next, he would smack me in the head and tell me to be careful not to keep doing that, because the eternal flames of hell would be waiting for me. Then, as "penitence", he would tell me that I should "pray" (I write it in quotes because what I really did is recite something that was automatically in my mind, without knowing its value) certain quantity of Our Father prayer and another bunch of Holy Mary prayers...

This did not happen only to me! It happened to thousands and thousands of people around the world and especially Mexico!

The most horrendous crimes in history of humanity have been perpetrated in name of "the religion". Let's take a very brief look towards the Middle East, where the "holy war" ends the life of thousands of human beings; let's remember the "holy inquisition" (I write it in lower case, since personally I am ashamed of this stage of the... catholic religion), while the most beautiful events in history have been, are, and will continue to be thanks to the spirituality we possess and the freedom we exercise when expressing love for every human being around us, particularly ourselves.

Despite of the above, I affirm that the human has a need to believe in someone superior and who good things that happen to us can be attributed to (and thanked for), or even to ask for the bad things to disappear or become good! It is perfectly common for us to convey events or objects a religious, magical, powerful meaning and use it for our tranquility, confidence and faith.

Living as a spiritual being without blockages or rituals with surname of religion represents opening the divinity we have, allowing that the authentic feelings surface before the smile of another human being, which in return, and without considering it too much, we embrace, we grant wellbeing, peace, tranquility and love in his or her life, and when leaving, we say: "God bless you", without religions, races, political tendencies, no gender or sexual preferences, everyone, everyone being part of an element, of a concert extraordinarily aligned with the Multiverse and that with confidence, this time with real confidence we can call: GOD!!!

Now, what does this have to do with the old aged? Well, something really very interesting and valuable: of every element I have mentioned and the ones that follow, this in particular is the last one that the old aged keeps at the end of his life. Have you noticed the amount of elders that visit the churches every day? Have you asked yourself why they spend hours with their rosaries praying, asking and imploring? Because it is their only alternative! They have not found response to their needs at their homes, with their families, with their friends… and those friends have been dying little by little. They feel like they don't have someone to turn to in many circumstances that happen every day, so they go to pray and plead, they cling to their beliefs, sometimes becoming fanatism.

Besides, with the absolute convictions that are borderline obsessive, they develop a terrible fear to death, but especially to what follows it: Hell! Purgatory! Eternal damnation! Suffering the "wrath" of God because of the sins committed! I ask you to put yourself in their shoes and perceive just a little bit of what they feel and fear, and understand the reason behind their temper, their ideas, their quirks, their behavior.

I have been called countless times to give medical consultation to elders that live "inside" the family. I get to the house and in a very kind way, and sometimes as an attention decorated with feelings that make me believe that come out of guilt, I receive comments such as:

– "Sorry about the mess... the maid didn't come today".

And we keep on walking around the house, then the garden, and then the utility room, which is where the grandpa or grandpas are. The medical consultation to the elder MUST be done taking plenty, many factors into account; several details must be observed, such as the location of grandpa's room, and what is kept there, besides a quantity of things that I am not going to mention in this space, as it is not the subject right now. In spite of what I just mentioned, I cannot go on without sharing another one of my observations: to go to grandpa's bedroom –the utility room–, you would have to walk through the garden, with a measly 40 watt lightbulb, and without protection or roof, in such a way that if it was raining there would be no way for grandpa to come to the main portion of the house without getting drenched, or if this happens during the night, without tripping and falling down.

One day, I was called for a medical consultation with the family's grandpa.

I entered his room, which was very dimly lit, and grandpa was almost constantly coughing. Beside him there were some cough medicines, two empty tea cups, his dentures in an almost empty glass and with plenty of marks because of the water that had evaporated; individual beds, chamber pots underneath both beds, one of them with old urine... darn it! Chaos!

I checked the sick grandpa with true love by introducing myself, listening to him and then checking him medically. Afterwards, as part of the ritual, I issued a prescription with some medications to be administered as soon as possible. I should mention that I handed the prescription to the grandpa, who gave it to his son, who had a kind face that was really as false as it could be.

The rest of the things I observed and thought have plenty of value, but I want to highlight that something called my attention very powerfully: a crucifix in grandpa's headboard and a calendar that was many years old, but with an image of Our Lady of Guadalupe. I returned and asked them (it was an old couple) what the reason of their faith was, or what was what they asked Jesus and Our Lady of Guadalupe for:

– "We expect them to remember us and deliver us from suffering and from making our sons and grandsons suffer".

THIS is what thousands and thousands of elders have left: the hope and faith of dying, because they don't have any goal, objective or anything else left that would keep them clinging to what plenty call "life". Is this living alive?

Their faith has been reduced to this. The rest of the elements I have mentioned and the ones that follow are non-existent: only to continue the habits and customs of plenty of generations before them they have left aside their own abilities and have saddled God or Virgin Mary with those responsibilities.

The spirituality is with us always. It is an element of life. However, we turn it into an element of irresponsibility, laziness, dependence, and pray for a very specific miracle: having money and health when we are old, but if we had enough faith in ourselves, we would do from our old age something worthy and filled with satisfactions, without letting our physical ailments being so important, and of course, breaking with the burdens that those poor and ancient habits mean, and that prevent us from growing. This would be the real miracle!

AUTONOMY

Autonomy, freedom... independence, what would you do without them? A human being with liberty or autonomy is more inclined to be happy, planning in a daily basis what to do the next day, with the absolute knowledge that there will be no restrictions beyond the obstacles established by distances, the time factor, the economical factor, among others, without following the indications, and in many cases, the orders of others. They are therefore always in the search of continuing with their plans.

The autonomy grants self-esteem and happiness, safety and comfort; it gives us the *power* to achieve everything we set our minds to; to decide, to break paradigms, to restart, to pursue the principles that have been established by ourselves, to trust, to distrust, to fear and get away or to feel safe and continuing; independence gives us the pleasure of choosing even what we should eat or leave aside, who to love or who to get away from, endure a situation or get away from it, and I repeat: it gives us the opportunity of *choosing* and not continuing with *consequences*.

Freedom is a determining factor for the self-improvement of every living being; being able to count on it creates mental and physical health, creates well being and encourages to express one's feelings, as well hidden as they may be, grants personal satisfaction, and therefore, as I already mentioned, self-esteem. The absence of independence or autonomy creates emotional pain, depression, diseases, and of course, death. What Victor Frankl mentioned in his book "Man's Search for Meaning" is true, and I take this opportunity to emphasize the point of spirituality described in the previous chapter:

"Freedom could be taken away from us, but never spirituality, which Is what makes life have sense and purpose".

Now is when I ask you: do old aged have freedom, autonomy, independence and free will to aim their steps and even desires or ideas? Definitely no!

I am referring to the case of those who live in their family's home, who establish a way of life for their grandparents and when they dare to contradict them, a series of situations come up, that could even make them end up in the doctor. In plenty of occasions, I observe that who takes grandpa for consultation asks me or tries to somehow make me aware of his desire of me backing up the impositions and restrictions that he has established for grandpa, such as his activities, the schedule for his meals and his bed time. I know that plenty of doctors accept this, probably because the one who pays is the one who takes grandpa for consultation...

PAUSE!: In the first place: who the f*ck does the doctor think he is to establish, prohibit and allow what the elder should eat, do or undo? And, who the f*ck do the relatives think they are to restrict the likings and pleasures, at least culinary to the father or grandfather, who is surrounded with so many limitations and has also so little time left to live?

The doctor who *orders* can go fu… have fun at the nearest park! But the doctor that suggests, advises, explains and not impose is ideal, and of course, welcome!

Another point: that part when they say *what is bad for him…* what do they base it on? Could it be based on those principles without fundament where they said that if they ate watermelon before going to sleep, they could get a bad case of diarrhea? Or that pork meat was bad for the heart? I will illustrate this some more: when I was studying my second year in med school, I already gave consultations –precocious kid– not at all! The thing is that I already had a daughter and her powdered milk was very expensive, and I had to work to get it. Anyway, I had my dispensary, where I gave consultations and medicines (medical samples that the laboratory representatives handed to those who promoted the medicines from their labs) for 10 or 20 pesos. I was one of those who charged 15 pesos for consultation and medicine. Mrs. Ortiz, after the consultation (come to think of it, she called me "doctor", and I was barely in my second year! Life is... funny!), well, as I was saying, after the consultation and the handout of the prescription and medicines, which I piled up over her sleeping child, while she held the prescription between her lips, she stopped, removed the prescription from her lips, and before leaving, asked: – "Doctor Valencia, should these medications be taken with a specific *diet*?". I tell you, for a second my underw... my pants fell down to the ground, and the first thing that came to my mind was: – "well, don't drink black coffee, black sodas, grease and hot spices". She immediately nodded and left the dispensary.

I was left there thinking in what I just did, and remembered that one of our teachers *prohibited* that same set of things.

Now I realize that it is a part of the ritual of the consultation and that the more medicines and more prohibitions the doctor prescribes, the better, as he will be able to charge more afterwards, and naturally, the relatives of the patient will say that he is "expensive, but very good".

As for me, I prescribe them maybe a medicine, a herb, I suggest that he doesn't drink milk (I will elaborate in this point later on) and for the relatives to satisfy the elder as much as possible in whatever he may ask, since... despite of all the medicines and restrictions he may be prescribed, he is going to die anyway! And if it happens, he is going to die happy! Let him choose his way of life and if he can endure it, his moment, place and way to die! (We will also speak further about this tough subject).

UNPAUSE: the other part of "he doesn't want or can't sleep", mmm... I ask myself: How the hell do you expect him to sleep if he spends all day napping in front of the TV? For this same cause, he wanders around during the night, because he is trying to find what to do, maybe trying to find a way of escaping home, which more than a home is a prison. Who knows what else!

I ask you again to walk in his shoes. This is the exercise of *compassion*, which does not have anything to do with pity; now I ask to you: –What would you do on his shoes? What would you do in a house where everything you do, say and think is dependent on the opinion of other members of the family, and even on other nosy people that just give their opinion without no one asking?

If you look after an old aged, let him live and even die as per *his* choices, and do not intervene, as you will get to a moment where you reproach yourself for having acted in any other way.

If you are in the case of being an elder under prescriptions, medical orders and even restrictions for any member of the family, consider that *no one* (relative, friend, priest, etc.) has the right to establish a way of living without quality for you, <u>let alone </u>a death without dignity or quality. Take control of your life, whatever your situation may be, and you will see what a pleasant sensation will flood your life and how many "diseases" will disappear.

Dare to do it, my friend!

SECOND PART

MY FIVE WISHES

This second part has been created taking a little –or a lot– from here and from there, and during my professional exercise I have found that this might be useful in the most precise way, but at the same time, it is subtle and prudent, and will allow me to present to those who grant me the privilege of reading this work, the most important stage of the life of every living being: his death.

I don't want to move on without mentioning something that has tickled my fingers for years now when I am before my computer and I decide to write something that is –according to my standards– important for every inhabitant of Mexico and the world, and I am referring precisely to the little importance that is given to old age and death, as we don't even care about preparing for any of these stages that are SO important in our lives; the importance given to this matter is SO scarce that the libraries do not promote –as I would like them to or as I think they should– books that have information on this subject; although it is true that an increasing quantity of dreamers (as myself or even more so) are in several ways working to spread the concept of *gerontoprophylaxis;* I can't help but noticing that a book about self-improvement, weight control, sexuality, etc. sells better, considering that when following the points described in this work, everything will come along, as this matter should not be dealt with only when one has already aged, but early in life, supported by the parents who have the vocation of being individual human beings, mature components of a mature couple, satisfied and with the common purpose of being parents. I tell you again: if we would insist in gathering the 12 points that I perfunctorily suggest here, your life would be totally different and not only would you live a happy old age, but a whole life in a perfectly and totally *alive* way.

I also notice how much the study and practice of thanatology has spread, which I consider very valuable, but, why not define with absolute precision what we want before, during and after our death?

To further clarify: we *believe* that we must leave our possessions; although, I'm against inheritances because in most of the cases, determining what and how much it is left to whom is the cause of ruptures, separations and things that are much, much worse. The contents of a phrase I use for conferences is very clear to me: *"if you don't fly first class, your inheritors will"*... this is, in the attempt (habits, customs, traditions) of inheriting and leaving to our successors the product of the work of all our lives, depriving ourselves from the satisfaction that means acquiring and enjoying what we can buy with money; I already mentioned this in the *Material Possessions* before. Even when my best advise is: spend everything you have, giving to yourself and enjoying that "buyable" thing you always wanted, there is something VERY important that you also have to leave as your wishes... final, previous, during and after your death: this is MY FIVE WISHES:

1.- Who will take the decisions when I am no longer in condition of doing so.

2.- The kind of medical attention I want and what kind I don't want.

3.- How comfortable I want to be.

4.- How I want people and family to treat me.

5.- What I want my loved ones to know.

1.- If you are no longer capable of taking decisions related to the caring of your health, it is advisable for you to name a person to take those decisions on your behalf. That person will take the decisions when and if these two situations occur: when my family doctor or the one who is consulting me determines that I am no longer capable of taking decisions related to my health AND if another health professional agrees with the primary physician. This person should preferably not be one of your sons, or members of the family, as there might be a discrepancy between them, and thus an estrangement might occur after this. The intention is that these five wishes put in written, as well as the *Anticipated Will* document (we will dig deeper into it in the following point), and preferably notarized, are both respected by the members of your family, as we are talking about your well-being and their tranquility; about taking away from them the tough responsibility of taking decisions when they are not prepared to do so, since we are not prepared to do so and do team labor, led in your favor by that person you have appointed.

2.- If you think your life is precious and that you deserve to be treated with dignity, when the moment comes when you're very ill and you are not even capable of speaking, maybe with irreversible brain damage, you should have already placed in written the indications that are related to pain control, to not having catheters applied or artificial nutrition set up through an unnatural tract; to not having medical respirators or cardiopulmonary resuscitation, transfusions practiced, dialysis or antibiotics: anything that has as objective keeping you alive, only with the minimal life support according to your personal or religious beliefs, and in the environment you consider your home. On this matter, there is a document that I have already mentioned, called Anticipated Will, which template I attach at the end of this chapter, so that, *with anticipation*, you print it, take it to a notary with witnesses, sign it and hand it to every member of the family for their clear and defined knowledge. Consider and make your loved ones aware that there is nothing more valuable than living with quality and dignity until the end, and of course, to consequently have a worthy, quality death, which details you defined clearly in that document. The most common thing to happen at this point is that each and every one of the relatives take decisions instead of the patient, especially those directed or suggested by the doctor, who in the purpose of prolonging the patient's life, only end up prolonging his suffering and that of the entire family. This is in no way euthanasia, but respecting and following the wishes of a person who is close to death.

3.- Also, you should write the following: <u>I don't want to feel pain</u>. My doctor will take charge of this regardless of me being a little drowsy; I want to be well cleaned, well dressed, and receive attention to my personal care, listen to my favorite music if possible until the moment of my death; I want to be read to out loud with passages with spiritual or religious content, according to my beliefs or religion. I want my loved ones, including children, to have the opportunity to approach me, to be able to speak to me as much as they want, and to receive the spiritual support they may need. I don't want the children, whether they are my infant children, grandchildren or any other close child to be lied to. I want him told that his presence is pleasant for me; I don't want people to speak softly thinking that I am not aware of the contents of their words and gestures. With this I wish to avoid a dismal environment to be created; one that is filled with fear, silence and darkness, since I consider that death is the most important part of life and life is a party, and therefore it should also be such at this moment.

4.- You should continue with the following: as far as possible, I do not want to be alone, especially when the moment of my death comes. I want to have my hand held, listening to your words, even when it may seem that I am not listening; I want to be treated with compassion, but not with sadness or pity. I want to have pictures of my loved ones in my room, close to my bed. I want to die in my home, as far as it is possible, as the best place to die is and will always be my home, surrounded by everything I love, especially those who I love and love me back.

5.- I want my family and friends to know I love them. May them forgive me if I somehow hurt them. I also want them to know that they have been forgiven when they thought they hurt me. I want them to know that I am not afraid of death, as it is the start of a new journey, of a new beginning of ME. I want every member of my family to make peace with each other, and to remember me as I was before the illness that brought me to my death, and for them to see my death as personal growth for each one of them. I want my body to be cremated ( ) buried ( ), and these persons know my wishes regarding my funeral: _____ and _____.

Once you have defined this, I can assure you that there will be plenty of peace in your soul; you will feel an exquisite sensation of tranquility, and it will increase the quality of life in your days.

It may seem to you like this document does not offer the guarantee of it being followed to the letter as per the redactor and signer's wishes: you are right. It could happen that who established and signed it suffered a fall, and a passerby called the ambulance. The "normal" protocol in medical unit to stabilize the patient at all costs, insert a needle with a bunch of solutions, a catheter and maybe intubate him to keep him "alive". If you notice this and you take the "My Five Wishes" document to the ER, it will not be good for nothing, as it is only valid for the family, but is not yet legally valid. This is why it should be notarized and protocolized. As an additional comment, I tell you that no hospital has the right of retaining a patient. You would only have to sign a voluntary discharge and you will be able to take your loved one to where he had chosen to be; for this you will be required to have a primary doctor to care for him according to the requests he recorded in the document.

Nevertheless, there could be the case where the consulting doctor refuses to do so and threatens you to charge you with "attempted homicide by privation of basic medical services", which does not have any legal foundations. It is a right you have, and even more so when holding this document. You will surely be frightened and let them do what they consider "necessary" to keep the patient alive, and of course, make some money while they're at it.

Given the above, I recommend you to reinforce the desire of your loved one, who manifested his wishes in written, and help him in the creation of a document called "Anticipated Will", which if not fulfilled as written, notarized, protocolized and registered, there will be some legal elements against those who oppose to do so. This document is included in the following chapter.

ANTICIPATED WILL DOCUMENT

The following is the template for the ANTICIPATED WILL DOCUMENT:

I.- INFORMATION OF THE REQUESTOR:

1.- Full name:

2.- Nationality:

3.- Gender:

Male   Female

4.- Place of birth:

5.- Date of birth:

6.- Name of the father:

7.- Name of the mother:

8.- Marital status:

Single   Married

9.- Address information:

Address:

(Street)   (Number)   (Apt Number)

(Suburb)   (Delegation)   (Zip Code)

Telephone:

Mobile telephone:

E-mail:

10.- Occupation:

11.- In the cases where the requestor is foreigner, Mexican by naturalization or son of foreigners, please fill the following form:

A.- IF HE IS A FOREIGNER

TEMPORARY RESIDENT Card number:

PERMANENT RESIDENT Card number:

Another immigrant status:

Attach copy of the document.

B.- MEXICAN

Document number:

Date of the document:

Attach copy of the document.

II.- PROVISIONS OF THE ANTICIPATED WILL DOCUMENT.

It is my desire to sign the ANTICIPATED WILL DOCUMENT, which will have the following:

1.- DESIGNATION OF REPRESENTATIVE

A.- Name:

(Name) (Middle name) (Father's surname) (Mother's maiden surname)

B.- Nationality:

C.- Place of birth:

D.- Date of birth:

E.- Marital status:

Single   Married

F.- Address information:

Address:

(Street)   (Number)   (Apt Number)

(Suburb)   (Delegation)   (Zip Code)

Telephone:

Mobile telephone:

E-mail:

Occupation:

2.- DESIGNATION OF THE SUBSTITUTE REPRESENTATIVE

If the abovementioned designated representative is not able to fulfill this designation due to his being discarded, revoked, is physically unable or has any other condition recognized by law, I hereby name a substitute representative:

A.- Name:

(Name) (Middle name) (Father's surname) (Mother's maiden surname)

B.- Nationality:

C.- Place of birth:

D.- Date of birth:

E.- Marital status:

Single   Married

F.- Address information:

Address:

(Street)   (Number)   (Apt Number)

(Suburb)   (Delegation)   (Zip Code)

Telephone:

Mobile telephone:

E-mail:

Occupation:

IS THIS THE FIRST ANTICIPATED WILL DOCUMENT YOU HAVE ELABORATED?

☐ Yes   ☐ No

If this is not the first one, please bring the last one you elaborated.

III.- COMPLEMENTARY INFORMATION

Concepts that need to be considered when granting the Anticipated Will document:

ANTICIPATED WILL DOCUMENT.- This is the public document, signed before a notary, in which any person with legal ability and in full possession of his mental faculties, states with the usage of his free will and full consciousness his serious request, unequivocal and reiterated, so that in the case where he suffers from any terminal disease, established by his family physician, he is legally able to refrain from undergoing through any medical or surgical treatment, or any other procedure that foster medical or therapeutic obstinacy, whether it is at home or at any medical unit, especially intensive care unit, as well as from prolonging life through any type of antinatural feeding means, such as nasogastric tube, or gastrostomy. In this document, he declares to formally accept his disposition to receive usual minimal measures and palliative and thanatological attentions, as well as accepting controlled sedation when the moment of death is closer.

TERMINALLY ILL.- This is what a patient with a terminal illness is called, or if due to circumstances beyond control, he has a life expectancy of less than six months, and cannot go on living in a natural way, based on the following circumstances:

a.- The diagnosis of the advanced, irreversible, incurable, progressive and/or degenerative illness;

b.- There is an inability of response to a specific treatment, and/or;

c.- Numerous problems and symptoms, secondary or posterior, are present.

MEDICAL DIAGNOSIS OF TERMINAL ILLNESS.- This is a document signed by the treating physician, who is registered before the General Direction of Professions and the Secretariat of Health, where it is specified that, posterior to the in-depth revision of the patient's medical history, and laboratory and specialized studies, establishes that the remainder of life of the patient is less than 6 months.

MEDICAL AND/OR THERAPEUTIC OBSTINACY.- The unnecessary usage of medical or surgical procedures to keep a patient alive when he is in terminal phase.

USUAL MINIMAL MEASURES.- These consist on providing hydration, hygiene, oxygenation, nutrition and/or curations to the patient that is in terminal phase, according to what has been established by the health and medical measures or protocols, without this affecting the patient's decision, and especially his dignity and quality of life.

PALLIATIVE AND THANATOLOGICAL CARES.- The active and total care of those diseases that do not respond to the curative treatments and that include the control of the pain and other symptoms, as well as psychological attention for the patient and the family.

CONTROLLED SEDATION.- This is the administration of medicines by the doctor that has been designated, or the family doctor, and the health personnel with the purpose of finding relief of the pain, unreachable through other means, of the physical and/or psychological suffering of a patient in terminal phase, with his explicit, implicit or delegated consent, without causing intentional death of the patient, and keeping him sedated, especially without pain.

REPRESENTATIVE.- This refers to the person or subscriber designated or appointed by the terminally ill patient to review and confirm the stipulations established in the Anticipated Will Document, with the purpose of verifying the exact and unequivocal observance of the points that were established in it, as well as the validity, integration and notifications of the changes that the patient decides to do to it.

SIGNATURE.- IT IS OBLIGATORY TO APPEAR BEFORE A NOTARY PUBLIC TO SIGN THE ANTICIPATED WILL DOCUMENT.

BOTH THE REQUESTOR AND THE DESIGNATED REPRESENTATIVE (ONLY THE FIRST REPRESENTATIVE: NOT THE SUBSTITUTE) HAVE TO BE PRESENT WITH A VALID FORM OF IDENTIFICATION (NATIONAL IDENTIFICATION DOCUMENT / MIGRATORY CARD OR PASSPORT).

Ask the notary/lawyer of your trust for the elaboration of the present document. Also, I would advise you for it to be handwritten by the requestor, thus absolutely emphasizing his desires.

In my opinion, this document represents a means that should be done in every family, and especially in those where there are vulnerable beings, with any pathology considered as high or medium risk, and grandparents. This will be wonderfully soothing for every member of the family, and particularly, for that person I am referring to, when knowing that a document with legal content that guarantees his desires for when the time comes has been established.

PERSONAL CONCEPTS REGARDING THE ATTENTION OF TERMINALLY ILL AND THE RIGHTS THEY BEAR

As I care for more and more sick elders and terminally ill people, I realize the amount of information and of course, misinformation that exists in this regard, and I don't want to go on without mentioning what I currently think, after witnessing incredible situations, precisely previous to the moment of death.

I definitely reject the usage of the word *"euthanasia"*. What is euthanasia? Dying well and in peace? Helping a patient die? Stopping any kind of vital or therapeutic support until the patient reaches his death in a "natural" way? I will leave aside the etymological meaning of the word only by whim, simply because after being present in the death of more tan 2,000 "patients" during 44 years of medical practice, and almost 40 exclusively with old aged, I have defined for me, in my personal practice, a very strict position, but absolutely based on love, on compassion, on humanism, on breaking the rules and those hypocritical judgements of those that because of guilty feelings ask me to extend life of their "loved" ones; I have decided many years ago to give the patient what *he* or *she* requires or asks for.

As you know, I don't only treat the patient: I treat the whole family as well, and this is why I notice his needs with plenty of detail; physical, medical, spiritual, psychological and even the position of his bed in relation to the cardinal points; I analyze the comments of each one of the relatives, carefully review how they are keeping him home, and in other cases in the cold Intensive Care room of any given hospital, I see and keep and thoroughly analyze his surroundings, his personal belongings, what lies on the nightstand beside him, if he has crucifixes or images of saints in his room, if he has a television or a flat screen (really!), as well as the controversies that each one of the members of the family express both non-verbally and verbally. After a while I cannot determine, as I don't use a watch, I integrate a diagnosis and define what I need to do.

My first approach with the patient, before all of the points I just mentioned is as follows: I sit beside him, I rub my hands against each other so that they are warm when I touch him, and then, while introducing myself, I ask his name, age, and other details, without letting the typical and overly stupid "how are you" phrase escape my mouth, ask him kindly to tell me what is happening, if he is in pain, what kind of pain and what is its intensity, and then I ask him how I can help him. I do all of the above while looking straight at his eyes and holding his hands, so that we establish physical and eye contact. I NEVER walk up to him and check his vital signs right away: never! I also never wear a gown (the gown, recognitions, diplomas and all of that twaddle does not make you a doctor), and I don't wear a tie either, as the seriousness of that marvelous first contact is established by humanism and love; the need of two human beings looking to communicate deeply. This becomes more important than the image of doctor that you could project.

In plenty of occasions, and I mean if the moment is correct, I ask him to tell me about his life, about what he used to do, what saddens him, what he fears... what he wants to keep and what he is willing to lose or leave behind.

Time is not relevant: once that this kind of contact with the patient has been established, the rest comes very fluidly, kind, comfortable, human, without obstacles of the protocolary or socially designed kind.

Then, the medical part comes along, and I assure you that you will not find a reactive hypertension, or tachycardia because "the doctor came to see me": you will explore the body that contains a human being who will gladly, kindly, cheerfully, lovingly and willingly allow you to perform the check up with the objective of giving him what he really needs.

Once you have established the diagnosis, checking all of his medical records, laboratory exams, specialized exams, etc., it is necessary to speak with the patient, and speak to him with sincerity, honesty and of course, tactfully to make him aware of what is coming or what could come. I tell him to ask me every question he may have, even if one of those could be "how long do I have?". Of course... of course I will never tell him that his life expectancy could be measured in time/hours/weeks/months... years! Never! This is the most anti-ethical thing that could exist. You could be a kickass doctor when it comes to removing appendixes or tumors, but you should never tell your patient that he has certain time to live!

These experiences are really extraordinary, wonderful and definitely enriching for everyone: family, patient and doctor! But they are especially humane, which is what the patient/teacher desperately wants and needs.

Taking his hands, kissing his forehead and asking him for permission to speak with the family must be the following step.

I ask as many family members as possible to sit down and speak, and after explaining as clear and understandably as possible what is going on with their loved one, AND without considering the time factor, I answer the questions they ask. Once that this has gone through with the utmost calm, I let them know the needs of their loved one: medical, humane and spiritual needs. I explain, according to the condition of the patient, what he really needs from all of them and I invite each one to go and speak to him asking for his forgiveness or everything they might have done that could have hurt him –whether it was intentional or not– and also forgive him for anything that may have caused damage or resentment of any kind –whether it was intentional or not–, and let him know that they love him, and as human beings that "coincided" in this Universal space to learn, we must understand that we all make mistakes.

This is truly wonderful, and I could write volumes to invite you and describe you what is going on inside the loved one that is in his process of death. In this precise moment, I only want to sensitize you.

Naturally, they ask me right away what I am going to prescribe, and my answer, of course, is conditioned to the condition of the loved one. What I never do or never will do is prescribe something that may extend his life when it does not have quality. If it is convenient, and according to the patient's requests, I administer an intravenous solution, and whatever he may need to control his physical, and naturally, emotional pain; I may indicate vitamins and highly nutritious food when I sense that he requires time to be able to detach from what is *tying* him to life.

In other cases or situations, I only indicate serum to keep him sensibly hydrated, I prescribe analgesics, as potent as they are needed, and apply a sedative in his intravenous solution to keep him rested, in peace and waiting his death.

If this is "euthanasia", I don't give a crap! I practice it! But I spend plenty of the so-called time talking to the patient close to his ear regarding his need of dying and accepting going towards his rebirth, to the other side... to the start of another journey, supported by all of those loved ones that are already waiting for him to help guide him to wherever he has to go.

NOBODY has the right to decide, design or define the quality and the dignity of life a patient must live with: the real *agony:* exists when the loved one in process of death does not know what to expect from those that surround him, including doctors, and naturally family itself; the most regrettable thing is that moment when in the deathbed, a member of the family approaches the patient and tells him: –"Please, mom, don't die! Don't leave me alone! I don't know what I would do without you!". Can you imagine what the patient feels and thinks?

Another common and equally detestable aspect is to keep the loved one in the intensive care unit when the likelihood of survival is null. The best hospital is where the heart is: home, surrounded by the things the patient love, being where he belongs, with his loved ones and not where he is not even asked permission to check his vital signs or to apply an injection; then the doctor comes, with his ego and totem face, asking how he is: the response, I'm sure, if he was able to express it properly, would be: –"how am I? Well, duh! I feel pretty messed up! Why do you think I'm here?

Practicing medicine or science in a terminally ill is cruelty, or *Dysthanasia*, using the terms that are utilized as justification. This means using every resource to keep someone alive without the quality of life or dignity being present.

For this last point, in the *My Five Wishes* section, I wanted to notarize these formats, so that they are legally and medically valid enough for you to remain calm to know that it is you who makes that call: nobody else.

I say to you again: I could write volumes and volumes about what the terminally ill patient has to receive, and what the family should grant to him; at this point I will limit myself to asking you a question: if you had esophagus cancer, with metastasis in many places of your body, with unbearable pain and you had a button in your hand that would result in your death if you pressed it, and therefore, you would rest of all of these things you are living/suffering, would you press it?

Every human being has rights that do not even appear in things such as the constitution, or that the bland or useless National Human Rights Commission does not contemplate, and some of them are the right we have to decide for ourselves where to live, how to live, where to die, and even how to die. If you don't agree, I would love to discuss it any time.

In uncountable occasions have I seen in the face and heard terminally ill patients filled with pain, say the phrase "please, end my life and my suffering". This has left a different sense to my professional/human life. This is why I have left aside the word "euthanasia". I do not practice resuscitation whenever an old aged dies. I profoundly respect that moment and lovingly accompany him until his heart stops beating and his soul sheds his body.

HEALTH

Now get ready for some innuendos!

In thousands of books, encyclopedias and in everyday life, the definition of health is something very simple at first sight:

"Health is the absence of any physical or mental ailment that could encumber the life of he who does not have it"

I ask: Is that it? Now I also ask: what is a disease? Could it be "the presence of physical or mental ailments that encumber the life of he who has it"?

Heck! I define myself as "paradigm breaker" and my most vehement intention in this work is sowing in as many people as possible the necessary consideration so that, in the earliest age possible an adequate plan is initiated so that your old age is the best one possible. It is very clear to me that until now there is NO such thing as the "golden age", "age of splendor" or "golden autumn or winter", just as it is described in these phrases; however, there ARE exceptional beings who climb mountains, form part of athletic events, marry with people that are several decades younger than them, and are just that: e-x-c-e-p-t-i-o-n-a-l! Nowadays, it is not possible to get to 80 years old without some ailments, product of excess of youth, with dental, auditory, motor and functional problems in every organ we have, and thus, give birth to some sayings, such as:

"Illnesses that come with the age".

"Everything wears out of service".

…And so many more, which contains the *acceptance* of the fact that we have to pay a price for living many years: our health has to be affected by the passing of the years. Once we have accepted this, *we decree* it as reality, as "normal".

Health in an old aged is intimately attached to its relation with a close and familiar environment, that can be considered as one's own, and that he feels part of, as happens with the needs that are satisfied by his own decision.

However, when talking about health in the elders, we immediately think about these factors: doctors, medicines, laboratories, X-rays, magnetic resonance, tomography, and a thousand other things, and this is what makes me think that we only take care of our health when something hurts.

When you go to the doctor, after seeing the results of the exams he "ordered", he gives you some medicines, a diagnostic with a name that is nearly impossible to pronounce, and asks you to go see a specialist in other branch of medicine that should be able to treat other or each one of the ailments you mentioned... each one of them will prescribe medicines and at the end, instead of having delicious sunny side up eggs, you will have to scoff down 12 different medicines for each <u>symptom</u> (not for the cause of those symptoms) you mentioned to the physicians! Oh, and so that they are soft on your gastric mucosa, have an Omeprazole...! Come on! I know you agree with me, since when their relatives tell me "my dad is not hungry", my first thought is: "how the hell is he supposed to be hungry when his stomach is filled with so many stupid drugs?

I have mentioned plenty of times: when grandpa gets sick, a member of the family takes him to the doctor and after a "professional protocol" in which the appointment is set 2 or 3 weeks later, even when they have space before, they get to the waiting room with medical magazines beside the uncomfortable chairs or couches, and after half an hour or more, the doctor shows up, who after a while checks grandpa, who by that time has a full bladder, and the hemorrhoids about to burst, in an office which walls are filled with diplomas and papers that DON'T tell what the doctor is, but where he has gone to, behind a huge desk that separates the "patient" from the doctor, who checks him with a "professional" face, without showing the faintest of smiles, which would give grandpa some confidence, and with the most stupid of questions: –"How are you, Mr. ...? What brings you here?" The only reply I would consider logical and understandable is: "Well, I don't feel good! That is why I came here, you idiot!" (Ok, not so rough, but something like that).

Then, the protocol: medical history, blood pressure check, respiratory and cardiac noises with the stethoscope, and then, after a while of listening to the complaints of <u>the relative that takes the old aged for consultation</u> and not grandpa himself, who wants to be heard in the first place, extends (in printed forms, provided by laboratories that give a cut to the doctor when he sends in patients) a long list of examinations that "have" to be completed.

More appointments will come, aggressions due to the lack of touch of those who take blood, X-rays or whatever the doctor prescribed. And then, it's back to him... the same protocol, appointment, waiting room, the showing up late of the doctor, and then... then, a prescription with a bunch of medicines, and... naturally... Omeprazole! Oh! I don't want to leave the huge list of prohibitions out, both in food as well as in activities, and even in the behavior of the "patient" ... this is what the current geriatric medicine is based on in most of the cases, with just a very few exceptions.

Oh! I was forgetting another restriction prescribed by the doctor! "No strong emotions, please". What would you say? I would say: not a chance! Life is made out of living emotions, and especially strong ones. Otherwise, there would be NO thrill at all in living it! If that would be the case, I'd rather die!

Health in us old men is determined by factors that were initiated many years before, when due to ignorance or habit we neglect the primordial factor at this point: the preventive medicine, or with other words, a basic component for *gerontoprophylaxis*.

Some years ago, I had an experience that I will share to you so that you can have a better idea on what the pharmaceutic industry represents worldwide, especially in the west.

While I was in Queretaro, where I went from Monday to Friday to direct a nursing home, an afternoon of a distracted day, agent John Doe, from a "world class" pharmaceutic company came to visit. Truth is that I didn't see him as an agent anymore, but as a good person who I could establish a friendship with, as we had already gone out for some drinks and dinner in a delicious restaurant in Universidad Avenue. After a formal greet and a warm hug, he handed me an envelope and said that it was a gift, and that he didn't want me to miss it. It was a courtesy for 3 nights and 4 days in an excellent hotel in Cancun, with all the expenses covered, including the cab, if I took one from my San Miguel to Queretaro's airport. – "Just keep the tickets"–, he said.

My immediate reaction was telling him that this was a trap and that the real purpose was to promote a memantine (medicine used in the treatment of the Alzheimer's disease). He responded that, regardless of the opinion I had on that medicine, this was a gift from him to me as a friend.

I decided to go.

Wow hotel! Wow meals! Wow drinks! Wow beach! Wow girls at the beach! Wow moments to think and meditate!

The last night, at around 8 in the night, I heard that someone knocked at the door of my room, and a bellboy, impeccably dressed, was waiting for me, with a jacket and a tie, as I was being expected for a meeting with two very important people in the best restaurant of the hotel, and of course, I should wear those clothes.

I came down the stairs with the jacket, the tie, trousers and tennis shoes! There were two elegant and impeccably dressed men, who left their glasses, stood up, and with exquisite kindness greeted me and invited me to take a seat. They told me to order whatever I wanted, and me, a little shy by nature (…), ordered Johnny Walker Blue Label… Booyah!

They introduced themselves as the international sales director of laboratory "X", and the national sales director of the same lab.

After a few minutes of toasting and talking about the weather, whisky, beautiful Cancun, if I had children, grandchildren, if I was married, etc., the national sales director said something like this:

– "Well, Mr. Richard Roe, as I already told you, Dr. Valencia, has been caring for old aged for many, many years now. He has written several books, gives conferences in some places, and I consider that having him on board would be a magnificent opportunity to launch our star product against the Alzheimer disease".

Smiles came and went... then, the international sales director, told me:

– "Yes, that is right. Mr. Jack Roe has been speaking to me about you for quite some time now and we decided to invite you so that we could make you an attractive offer. If you allow us to place our lab's logo, and of course, the commercial name of our memantine in the back cover of the book you present annually in FIL, in your event FIL'Abuelos, we are authorized to hand you a monthly quantity of $..., but it you let us place publicity in your conferences where the attendees can see it, and a small stand where we are able to promote our product, that quantity could go as high as $..., additional to the other quantity, plus vacations twice a year for two for one week or ten days to any place in the world, with all the expenses covered.

Darn it! I perceived the emphasis he put in the word "all"! The zip of the delicious whisky did not feel rough on my throat! I was only able to be surprised by the reaches that the pharmaceutic industry is willing to go to convince the doctors to prescribe something that... well, I won't comment on this, as it is not the subject of this work. However, I must say that I declined the appealing proposal. I only told them that if their product is so "good and effective", why would they resort to those kinds of advertisements. We said goodbye, with an "I will think about it" from my part (I had already made up my mind, but I wanted to be polite), and from their part with a "see you soon" ...

This is an example of what the pharmacologic industry offers to all of us. Given the above, I ask you the following question: do you trust *totally* in your doctor and in the medicines he prescribes?

I graduated from Medical School from University of Guadalajara. As far back as I can remember, I have wished to be a doctor. There was an exception during elementary school, in my sixth year, where professor Oliva and Escuela Cervantes's principal ("escuela", as in "school for children with parents with limited resources", and not as in "Colegio Cervantes", another school in my hometown), Mr. Mendoza, influenced me to become a priest or a Marist teacher. Can you imagine me as a priest or as a Marist teacher? Nooooo! Then that period of time was over and I kept on my illusion of being the best neurosurgeon in the world!

Ever since I can remember, I was also interested in getting to know how the human body works. I first caught some mice, which I checked their interiors (...). Then I caught some cats, which were "sacrificed in the name of medical science", and then dogs: please do not criticize me; as I write this I feel bad... poor animals! But then, more than one made it out alive and kept on living. I learned a lot in junior high with my friend Victor Antonio Fuentes Vazquez, and then in high school, I bragged about my abilities as surgeon.

I tended to my first birth when I was 18 and... and they called me "doctor" You cannot imagine how nervous I was! But with some luck, everything was ok.

I have already met the grandchildren of the first kid that used me to bring him to this world. Heck! We're getting old! I though when I met him.

Maybe because I had the best grades, with the best grade average in the high school, I was admitted without any difficulty to the School of Medicine, Surgery and Obstetrics. I was so happy! I was so honored!

When I finished studying I had already gotten married, I had a gorgeous daughter and the need to provide: I arranged the garage of the house we were living in and I transformed it into a waiting room, and a space I can't remember what was for later became my office, with desk, with my diploma and some recognitions of the courses I have attended, some ornaments and whatnot. Obviously, I wore a white gown!

I listened to my patients' ailments, and then I would start to form the shape of their illness and naturally, I would then prescribe some medicines. Then, I would examine them carefully, I checked what later would become routine, and at the end of the appointment, I would jot down the names of some medicines that I felt or believed would do them good. Most of the time, they got better, or got back with the same ailment, with some more… and then I charged (this has been the most difficult part of my career: charging). I would walk him to the door, gazing at the people that were sitting on the benches I had made myself, and said out loud:

– "Who is next?".

And then the next patient would step in my office, and the story would repeat itself.

Now I practice a *different* kind of medicine. I am not the best neurosurgeon, not even neuro or surgeon (I almost do not perform surgeries anymore, sometimes I suture the underpants that have torn using my surgical material… or I sometimes sew buttons to my shirts). (hahaha… to shed some color to this moment, I will share that while watching the Inspector and the Pink Panther cartoon, I began to reinforce the buttons of my shirt, and when I was done, I noticed that the "suture" had also reached my underwear and the bedsheet I had on my lap... hahaha!). I do not consider the patient as patient anymore, but as a being with needs, and being listened to is the first in the list. I do not wear the white coat, or the stethoscope around my neck, nor do I have the lustrous office with innumerable diplomas covering its walls, or a desk, or the plenty of gifts that the lab representatives do when visiting us to promote any given allopathic product. I visit my patients at their homes, where I know how they live, how they feel, the way they receive attentions or cares from their families, significant others or friends, or no one! I don't have, obviously, a waiting room, and I seek to be overly punctual when visiting them.

I don't use a watch, since, when checking it, it would be like if I was rushing them while listening to them while they narrate pieces of their lives to me. Who is truly privileged in this doctor-patient role is me! After listening to them without limiting their time, I examine them, ask a lot of questions, not only related to the medical aspect, but also to their situation in their lives, their plans or goals, their dreams, aspirations, feelings, relations with their family, their friends or society, with people of the opposite gender, etc., etc. Then, I ask them about their physical ailments, since I, by that time, already have a good idea of their emotional ailments.

Next, I *suggest* what I consider best for them in the subtlest way, but showing security and experience.

Enough about me! What I want to emphasize is that the health of the old aged nowadays is not determined by the attention to their physical or emotional ailments, but by the stupid quantity of medicines that are prescribed to continue with a medical ritual in which the old man attends to the doctor's office, taken by the "primary caretaker", and may this be understood as he who pulled up the shortest straw on the *necessary* responsibility (I know thousands that take this as a burden) of taking him to the doctor after grandpa complained repeatedly of plenty of ailments of every kind to the doctor, whatever his specialty may be.

I want to make a pause regarding medical specialties: in other times, the doctor was "general" and saw every member of the family, knew everyone perfectly well, and the same thing happened when he saw people from a town or small city; he could treat someone from tonsillitis (and operate them), or treat someone from indigestion; everything from circumcisions to natural births and caesarean sections. He cared for people that had been wounded by a firearm, or just an FSB (freakin' strong hit); he attended the houses of his patients and they first spoke about several subjects, such as the weather, the harvest, or the current president, and then he was told about the ailments that the family's "sick" person was suffering from. He would see him, and prescribe Vic's VapoRub in his chest, neck and back, ginger and cinnamon based syrup, sweetened with honey. Sometimes, he would even prescribe hot coca cola for the cough, penicillin, and then he would collect at the end. Most part of the payment consisted in cash, and the rest in kind, with things such as a piece of meat, a live chicken or sometimes a chopped chicken (already dead, of course (parenthesis within the parenthesis... I'm laughing of my wisecracks) or a bottle of mezcal). One day, I was given a pig, and some other time, a turkey, both alive! There were no specialties. In that time, there were no medical *specialties*.

One day, my already deceased friend Raul Bravo –excellent aquarellist and author of some books such as *"Bolitas de Naftalina"* and *"Prohibido Aburrirse"*, among others – was telling me that the future of the medicine would be established in ridiculous specialties, such as being otorhinolaryngologist, but specialized in the right ear, and another one specialized in the left one.

Because of what I mentioned in the preceding lines, I don't want to disrespect those who spend hours studying with the purpose of obtaining a "more special" specialty to serve better, no! What I do want, what I intend to say is that as one dedicates more time and energy to knowledge, the humanism that every doctor has should NOT be lost. Doctors should also *get involved* with their patients and their relatives, because, and I reiterate once again: *in a family where the sick one is grandpa, the rest of the family is sick as well.* Please, doctor, don't "despecialize" in that what should be your main trait: love and humanism for the patient, since, besides of him being the object of your decision and illusion for being a doctor, he is your real teacher, and then "specialize" in being the tool he requires to heal his body and... his soul, of course!

And especially, you, who goes to the doctor seeking for help, why don't you demand what you deserve? Why do you receive and settle with the same thing always? Do you have the idea of who benefits who in this doctor-patient relation? It is the doctor who benefits from it, and not because of the professional fees you pay to him, but because you granted him your trust to be treated by him! Asking a doctor for him to treat you is you granting him a privilege! Therefore, *demand* to be treated how you deserve: these situations have gotten to a point where you get mad because you have allowed it!

My question, after all of this drag, is, where does the old aged or elderly fits? Who should look after him? The general surgeon, the otorhinolaryngologist, the gastroenterologist, the neurologist, the psychiatrist, the gynecologist (women, of course), the internist, the cardiologist, the orthopedist, the pneumologist, the ophthalmologist, the neurosurgeon, the proctologist, the urologist, the nephrologist, the endocrinologist...? Who? Well, the geriatrist, of course! He is a combination of all of the above. Ah! But then there are some other fields: the psychogeriatrist, the psychogerontologist, the gerontologist...! My goodness! What a chaos!

And why is that absurd need to resort to someone that has diplomas, masters and doctorate degrees and what not... and not resort to a "listener with integral knowledges of the total needs of the elders"?

Enough criticism... well, I still have some, since, in previous lines I mentioned, I would like to awaken the desire in you to be treated in a different way or demanding that your elder is when you take him to the doctor: when the family grandpa "feels sick" (let this be read as: feels lonely, isolated, without the attention of the rest of the family), he complains about something and calls himself "sick", which is why he is taken to the doctor (I have already told on him a thousand times) and after a long while, the doctor attends him in the *waiting room*, checks him and emits a diagnosis: "he has to take these lab tests to find the origin of his illness" who, while watching the results without smiling and with "professional" face, says with a heavy look and voice:

– Mr. (John Doe) has "problems that are typical and normal of his age", and if he does not take the medicines that I have prescribed, or if he does not follow my indications, it is very likely for him to develop an acute... (something that ends in "itis") and then he could die after a long period of suffering. This is why he needs the following...".

And then he starts jotting words that mean medicines, 10 or 12, or maybe more, the dosage and over all, the *restrictions*! He should not eat this, that, or make any strong effort or emotions, this is, NO strong emotions... and at the end of this consultation, can you imagine (put yourself in the shoes of grandpa) what he is feeling and what he would like to yell? Scumbag doctor! He has condemned me to *live dead*, he has taken away everything I have wished for only because I have wanted to be a member of this family, because I have wanted to be *present*! Why would I want to live like this?

I have mentioned this before. I just want to emphasize it more.

...The health, for God's sake... the health! In my life as "traditional doctor", meaning, I wore a watch, a coat, used an expensive branded pen, a desk, a waiting room and had a beautiful receptionist with an extraordinary body (I miss Chata!). I did all of the above rigorously... and I felt "professional" like that.

Yes: we are in the hands of the laboratories all around the world. To "lower the cholesterol", one of the statins (I will not mention brand names out of respect to your goals and aspirations and especially to those who take them convinced that they are the "best"); to lower the blood pressure, you will need to take for life (...) beta adrenergic blocker (quite a name, huh?), and the truth is that, if you take it, you will have troubles getting an erection... which will definitely mess up your night! Well, if you're a guy... An aspirin every day of his life... and one day, –bad day, of course– he dies because of a bleeding in his digestive tract, caused by the freaking aspirin... Well, I may have sounded a bit dramatic, but surely, he will start getting bruises (the correct word is "petechiae", in plural) in his arms, legs, buttocks and other geographic spots of his body. I have met people that for many, many years have been taking 500 mg of aspirin every day because his doctor asked him to do so for the rest of his life!

There are NO allopathic medicines without side effects: NO! What is "funny" is that the geriatric patient takes at least 5 medicines and even 12 in the breakfast, lunch and dinner... oh! And ranitidine or Omeprazole to "avoid the gastric irritation caused by that polypharmacy in his stomach". Can you imagine the accumulation of all the side effects of all those medicines together? My next question is, how the hell do you want your grandpa or old aged to be hungry when he has his belly filled with so many "products of the medical science to alleviate his ailments"?

I forgot to mention that Omeprazole has such a long list of side effects that you would be surprised if I mentioned it. It's enough to mention that it interferes with the processes that lead you to have an at least healthy memory. Taking a daily dosage of 40 mg of this "medicine" during long periods of time, (3 to 6 months) has caused memory issues that have been diagnosed as "senile dementia" (this is what their relatives tell me, as this has been the doctor's opinion).

I could enumerate, with some fear of disappearing mysteriously from this world, the side effects of every medicine your grandpa takes, or you at this moment! But there are things that are more important, and that I must present to motivate you to be really strict when taking any medicine prescribed by any doctor of any specialty.

I will share with you something that happened to me some years ago.

My blood pressure is always normal. Due to my excesses while using my strength when lifting the residents of the nursing homes I served in for many years, I had to have a surgical procedure in my lumbar spine, and then in my shoulder, and then in the other one, and something happened before and during the surgery that made my blood pressure spike to 240/140 and a little bit more.

Driven by my doctor's advice, I went to the cardiologist, and after many exams, I was diagnosed with "sudden death syndrome". From that day on, if I went on a trip, I could maybe forget my underwear, but never my medicines... and the years went by with those medicines, until I noticed that, when driving on the highway during the night, I saw halos of light of every color around the headlights of the cars that were going in the opposite direction, and this obviously scared me. This was caused by a medicine called amiodarone, which controlled my cardiac rhythm. That night I had a deep thought, and I decided not to take any medicine for my hypertension or for my cardiac rhythm, as for that time, I recommended coconut oil, gingerbread, curcuma, seeds such as chia, sunflower, pumpkin, quinoa, etc. for plenty of the ailments of my patients, so I threw the medicines to the trash, and from that moment on, I take two spoons of virgin or extra virgin organic coconut oil, green tea, gingerbread tea, curcuma tea, cinnamon tea, and guess what?

My blood pressure is always normal and my heart has a Tapatio and San Miguel rhythm! In other words, happy and calm!

I must confess that I am the most sceptic doctor in the world, and that I always rejected everything that was not allopathic, patent medicine, along with their complicated names, in such a way that when somebody approached me and told me that homeopathy cured asthma, I definitely rejected it, as I said, knew, felt, and was taught that it could not be cured with anything! Cortisone, bronchodilators and even antibiotics were my arsenal and… it was not cured! It only got better, but only for a short time.

There was a day when I met a herbalist, who was willing to bet that he could cure asthma in a 34-year-old patient who I had treated for a year. I challenged him. He attended him. He healed him! He gave her several teas, did several procedures I could not understand, and after two days, he told me that she had been cured. Obviously, I did not believe him at all! But up to this day, I have not seen that patient again for her asthmatic problem.

This sowed the seed of doubt in me.

It would take several pages of this book to describe to you all the experiences I lived during the months and years that followed, but I will just sum them up with the following: an entrepreneur friend from Guadalajara, who I was talking to about the reason so many Mexicans decide to go and try the "American Dream", the way they suffer so much, and their tremendous experiences, and talking about the reasons behind people that buy their products taking advantage of them, about the poverty of the farmers, and we then started talking about herbalism and alternative medicine; by that time I had already read plenty on the matter, and we agreed to do a world congress of integrative medicine, which would be an event where the medical alternatives that could provide quality of life at a reasonable price would be spoken about. Also, the focus would be helping those who sow and sell medicinal plants in an effort to avoid their emigration to the north, and all of the consequences this implies.

And so, I got in touch with doctors, healers, shamans of every field, coming from plenty of places in Mexico and, the world! What I learnt from them left a mark in me that has lasted until this moment of my life! And of course, they sowed the seed of doubt of the veracity and effectiveness of all of those medicines I had been prescribing for so long!

I got to know acupuncture, the ayurvedic medicine, the traditional medicine of China, Cuba, Mexico, the coyote medicine (I bet you didn't know about this one!), the usage of medicinal marihuana, I learnt the real sense behind things such as "empacho" (traditional term used in Mexico for a type of indigestion), "fright" sickness, the reason behind lifting the skull to the baby if he had it sunken, I learned about the Mexican thistle... and just as an example, for patients with Alzheimer, I prescribed a medicine which cost was at least $3,000 current pesos, and that is good for nothing! And with one kilogram of that herb, with a cost of $60 pesos per kilo, properly prepared, it was possible to avoid the cognitive deterioration in those same patients, and for a measly sixty pesos per kilo! I met Chaya Michan, Erick Estrada from Chapingo, Dr. Claudio Carvajal, Dr. Hector Solorzano, a shaman that could tell you if someone had cancer only by their odor... wow!

I got to know techniques of adjustment of vertebrae, knees and other bones that allopathy tried to fix with surgery, anti-inflammatory medicines (that destroy the stomach) and other "top-notch medical novelties", and with those techniques that took no more than half an hour, the patients walked out of the doctor's office... Weeeeell (again, as my editor Claudia says), this forced me (to serve better) to get to know more and more, to read, to call, to ask, and question everything I considered "medical science" up to that moment. I had neglected the sacred principle over which the real medicine is based upon:

The real healer is NOT the doctor, but the patient himself.

I very proudly quote something that I read many years ago, I forgot afterwards, and that I recently remembered. I'm talking about something Voltaire had said some while back:

> *"The art of medicine consists in distracting the patient while his own nature cures him".*

Of course, what the bearded guy Hippocrates said, also called my attention:

> *"Let medicine be thy food and food be thy medicine".*

Damn!

Then where is the disease? The health? Then, if somebody is "sick", then why the hell should we take him to the doctor, if he can be cured by himself?

In the ancient societies of the world, there was a doctor who treated, healed or battled all the alterations of the internal balance and the relationship with the environment, with the social or family group of one of the populators, which was manifested as a "disease". He used herbs, chants, massages, secret potions, all of these obtained by natural means and from nature, managing to achieve the restoration of the "patient's" wellbeing. My question is, nowadays, why do nowadays we go see a doctor, someone who after plenty of years of studying, with a very respectable medical science recognizes that imbalance in his patient and gives it a name that was established years ago, maybe plenty of years ago, something like fever (medically speaking, "hyperthermia") because of a tonsillitis? He prescribes antibiotics and naturally, medicines to lower the fever. I cannot carry on without mentioning how much these two preceding points make me wonder: the fever presents as a natural response of our organism before an aggression of maybe a bacteria; that raising of our core temperature indicates that the defense system of our bodies is producing elements that fight against that aggression, and then we are prescribed paracetamol! Yes, the fever will drop, but it will be breaking the functioning of the defense system of our wonderful body! Voltaire himself (I consider this guy a real genius; his contributions were extraordinary and was overshadowed by history and by "modern" science), as I was saying, Voltaire said that if he had a way of controlling the temperature of the human body, he would have the ability of curing every existent disease.

Is it so true that a measly bacteria that requires the usage of a microscope to say hi to it is capable of ending the life of a human being, who according to the Bible, is God's masterpiece? Are we really that screwed?

I know, I know, I'm getting you in plenty of trouble... I have been there thousands of times! But this is SO settled in our minds that I remember my mother telling me that if I stepped on the floor with my bare foot I would get tonsillitis! And if the tonsils keep swelling they need to be removed, even when they form part of the first and powerful element of your body, that can heal you from what has attacked you if you allow them to act? Why are we born with them, if some day we are going to need to have them removed?

Haha, I don't have tonsils (they were removed by Doctor Sergio Sanchez Cesena), or appendix, because the doctor said that in those days they both had to be surgically removed for my own good. Thank God I didn't have any flea bite in one or both of my testicles that could have later evolved into an infection, because otherwise I would not know how to explain to myself that my sons are my sons!

Then another thought popped into my mind, which reinforces the contents of the preceding paragraphs: What about our nature, made to God's image and likeness? Is it really SO fragile?

While pursuing my personal dreams, my patients' teachings, their relatives' teachings, and of course, because of the love I have had for medicine ever since I can remember, I stuck to every principle that was published in plenty, plenty of books I have read, and to my teachers' teachings; I devoured articles that appeared before me seeking to be the best doctor, but the time came when I asked to myself: does being the best doctor implies snatching from the "patient" his right to finding the cure of his ailment –whatever it could be– by his own means, or in other words, without consulting anyone, but only resorting to the faith he had owned until the moment I hand a prescription and tell him that he has to depend on those medicines to improve his health? Until giving him a list of prohibitions even though I don't have any idea why? Just to follow the medical protocol?

I don't forget that, when I was barely 20 years old, I already had a medical dispensary in 1634 Los Maestros Av., in Guadalajara, where I collected medicine samples from several places and consulted patients (barely 20 years old, and they called me "doctor" ... this blew up my ego, of course) and I charged $15 pesos for the consultation and the medicine. The patient walked out with his prescription and a bunch of medical samples in his hands. One time, one of the most frequent patients I had, asked me before walking out:

– "Dr. Valencia, does my treatment need a special diet?".

In a fraction of a second, I did not know how to answer. Luckily, it came to my mind what I once heard from one of my teachers and answered:

– "Yes, don't take coffee or spicy food. Don't eat pork meat, food with plenty of fat or dark sodas.

I laugh so hard at this right now, as she finished my advice with a:

– "I should also avoid chili and irritant foods, right?

Is this medicine? Generating dependencies? Restrictions? Creating or generating faith (I recently heard that faith is 90% doubts and 10% hope, but anyway…) in a measly capsule that contains, after a pharmaceutical process, the same that you can find in nature, even in your house's backyard?

Do you happen to know that coffee is an excellent antioxidant and that can help prevent many of the so-called diseases? Do you know that pepper –considered a condiment– is an excellent activator of metabolism and activator of other antioxidants that should be part of our daily meals? Do you know that pork meat is actually cleaner than chicken meat? Do you know that fat is elementary for our health? Something that will shock you: if someone before your eyes suddenly takes his hands to the chest and reports an unbearable pain at heart's height or in his left arm, or even in his back, you could be witnessing an acute heart attack. Did you know that could save his life with a quarter of a teaspoon of cayenne pepper under his tongue? Same happens with crushed red pepper (arbol chili pepper). I can assure you that he will be fine with time to get to an ER to continue his treatment. But be warned: he will leave with swollen lips and a cataract of snots caused by the chili burn he just went through… but you saved his life!

Plenty, plenty more to be detailed in another part of this book, when we get to talk about diet and food.

I read somewhere something I love, which I already mentioned, and which I keep in my mind always for reasons you can imagine, and which I repeat it now:

"*We are spiritual beings living a human experience*".

Then, why have we left our ability to exert that spirituality behind? That faith in ourselves, in the *healer* that lives within us and that could work towards our physical and mental well-being?

I lived another experience in April 7th, 1977, when we lost my dear brother Vicente in the sea. I was with the mother of my sons (already with my loved first born) in Garcia de la Cadena, Zacatecas, as she had been assigned to that place to fulfill her professional social service, and I was reluctant to leave them in that place by themselves, when at 3 o'clock in the night, her brother and uncle came to the health clinic we were in. After a bit of stuttering, they told me that Vicente had gone into the ocean (Playa de Oro, near Miramar and Manzanillo) and he had not come out yet... darn it! That day, I was sick with the worst bronchitis I can remember. I coughed constantly and it tasted like blood. I had fever, pain all over my body, but after I had heard that, I got dressed, put on a thick jacket, since, even though it was April, the weather was very cold, or that was how I felt it, and headed back. I rode in the back of a pick-up, or in other words, out in the open... after 5 hours, we arrived to Guadalajara, and I hugged my mother, who had the most painful expression of pain I had ever seen in a human face. She said to me:

– "Son, your brother is lost at sea. Go and get him back, for the love of God".

I was the first of 11, and in an "automatic" way I accepted the responsibility of looking after every one of my brothers. There was a time when I even considered them my sons. So I jumped in my car, with my father and one of my brothers, and we immediately went to Manzanillo to obey my mother's orders, since I had promised to her that I would bring Vicente, my son, back. My dear reader, I am crying as I reminisce... I am sure you understand.

Just as we got to Ciudad Guzman, we went to the house of a half-brother of my mother to call home and to ask if there were any news. No, there weren't. But something happened that moment: "I noticed that there was no cough, or fever, or mucus, or anything from that stupid acute bronchitis or pneumonia that was bothering me some hours ago! What happened? Well, something elementary: my internal *healer* eliminated that "illness" to give me all the energy and ability to face that situation, which was so, so painful! I focused ALL of my attention in driving at full speed so that I could meet with my beloved brother and take him back to my mother!

We reached Playa de Oro: open sea, in the beach, a bathing suite that belonged to my brother Vicente, a pair of sandals and a box with date fruits... I looked towards the sea, and I had the feeling I would never see him again. That is what happened: we never recovered his body.

What came after is not the point I want to share with you, since, despite that event being so painful, weeks after, I came to notice what I just told you about my bronchitis and how I was healed. This made me think that when you require that *healer* everyone, and I repeat: everyone has inside, it will surely wake up and act to provide the support, relief or energy to pull through. I hope that if you require from your internal healer, it is not under such dramatic or intense circumstances as the ones I just shared.

I need a break... I will pick up where I left tomorrow.

Every day, I dive into internet seeking for explanations to my questions and I had the immense fortune of finding Dr. Bruce Lipton with his book "The Biology of Belief", with a wonderful crazy thought:

"Thoughts are more powerful than diseases".

He also mentions that:

"Thoughts are more powerful than any medicine".

Yes! He is totally right! This is what I have based many years up to the present moment! Why Don Raul Ramirez, author of one of the books I presented in the first FIL'Abuelos event in '99, after being in the ICU with a life expectancy of no more than 48 hours, once I showed him his book, and left it at his feet on his bed and told him that I would be waiting for him on Sunday at 12 in our beautiful and transcendental event for its formal presentation (this happened on a Thursday and he had all the cannulas, catheters and medical equipment connected to him) got up and punctually showed up stumbling and with happy tears in his face on December the 2nd at 12 to proudly show his book "Poems of an Old Poet"? Why? Because he told his scientific "life expectancy" or his life doctor to go to hell, and received one of the most powerful motivations of his life. His sons told me between tears that after I visited him at the hospital, and showed him his book, he started to say and insist that he wanted to be discharged, until he obtained a voluntary discharge and went to accomplish one of his life's dreams. His presentation was more than dramatic: after I gave a pause for the public to get a rest, 5 minutes before 12 o'clock of that December the 2nd, the doors opened, and just as dramatically as it happens in the movies, the public started to make way for a man: a human being not so tall, a little overweight, his face covered in tears, while he walked the almost 20 meters that separated the doors from the presidium. With his right hand, he asked me for the microphone, and looking at my eyes, while his back faced the crowd, who rushed to occupy their places, he said to me:

– "Thank you, doctor, thank you. You have made me such a happy man when I finally saw a book I had so much desire to present... I cannot go on, because my throat hurts from all of the tubes I had back at the hospital, but thank you for giving me life and this joy. God bless you! Son"– he turned to his son, who had his face soaked in tears of joy, and told him: –"please take the book and present it. I am very tired".

The rest happened magically, unforgettably, simply beautifully, and in a VERY human way. His son did not stop crying while presenting the book of Don Raul. Nor the attendees.

Wow! So, are we or aren't we a bit divine? Yes, yes, we are! And in a regular and protocolary way, by habit, as it is "established", we go to the doctor and we expect orders to define a way of life, a diet, and especially, the order to take so much medication. All of this makes us forget the ability we have to generate our self-healing, we decree the *dependency* of doctors, their advises and the medicines.

I could narrate plenty of cases where what is known as miracles happen, but they are only manifestations of the rebellion of some to follow those so-called prescriptions that are part of a protocol and especially part of a financial ultra-phenomenon of several billions of dollars: the pharmacological industry. Then, where is the disease and where is the health?

According to what I have said in the preceding lines, we could come to the conclusion that *there are no diseases*, but only people that *believe and accept being sick*, caused by the more than wide spreading in every means of communication of so many symptoms, medicines to treat them, the presence of so many types of cancer, syndromes, diseases with weird, hard to pronounce names, and that most of them cannot be cured. I hear comments from some people I meet at a party (we cannot avoid being labeled as "doctors" wherever we go) and tell me that they have fibromyalgia or Guillain-Barré syndrome, or GERD (gastroesophageal reflux disease) and plenty, really, plenty names which cause is practically impossible to remember, let alone their treatment, precisely because of the *belief* that they are diseases and that getting sick is "normal" among us.

I notice in all of those people intelligence, culture and maybe plenty of curiosity for knowing what their doctor gave them as diagnosis, and of course, the positive effects, the not-so-positive and the side effects of each one of the medicines they were prescribed.

In a separated paragraph, I want to mention that not all that you read on the internet is true, and that if you check if the medicines that were prescribed to you will really cure you, you will surely doubt everything: diagnosis, medicines, and even the doctor, and this is why I strongly suggest that you fully trust your doctor, because otherwise you will not put your faith in what he prescribed. Oh, but you need to adequately *choose* the doctor you consult, as it could result even fatal not to.

THE DISEASE

I totally agree: the disease exists, whether it is real or we just think it is; the fact is that we suffer alterations in the balance and harmony that we should keep in each one of our organs, and therefore, we should not leave aside the *real* phenomena that happen to us from almost our birth, and that definitely are part of a process we call *aging*.

Every disease is an inflammatory process, as well as progressive, resulting from the oxidation of organs and their functions because of the adherence of a radical or molecule of free oxygen and *oxidizes* them. The accumulation of these oxidizing processes are the ones to lead us to suffer from alterations in the functioning of the organ or organs affected, and then, if really important factors, such as attitude, emotions, thoughts and stress, we will end up living this so-called disease, from a simple flu to the most devastating of cancers.

This is the oxidizing stress.

For any disease to appear, many of the mentioned factors need to be present. Otherwise, it won't happen.

Let's see the case of a bacterial invasion.

We all know that plenty of bacteria dwell in our skin, our digestive apparatus and for some reason, they don't damage us, until a determinant element emerges and allows these bacteria and their toxins to pass to the circulatory stream, or in the same place where up to that moment they exist in and cause superior damage to the one that our defenses can control.

I imagine in a way that may seem funny to you a group of Escherichia coli bacillus having a chat one day in a corner of an intestinal loop in the light of a lightning bug our patient swallowed alive, some of them smoking, others eating food residues that pass along, and others a little bit drunk for the alcohol residues they find passing by without being absorbed.

The *alpha* Escherichia coli says:

– "Hey, what if we stop by and go for a swim in the circulatory stream of this guy in whose guts we live in, and we find a new home in an organ to live out of it?"

The rest scream in unison:

– "Let's do it!".

And so, they decide to do it. BUT, what obstacles will they need to face to be able to accomplish their plan?

One VERY special on the side of the patient: the *belief* or lack thereof that the bacteria is superior to the human being. And the *conviction* that the medicines will cure the disease or alteration of health they produce.

It is simply not possible to wipe or leave aside in one blow what has been sowed in all the human race regarding the "virulence" of certain bacteria, virus and a bunch of bugs with names so funny already that we get sick only by trying to pronounce them. It is also not possible for you to, after reading this book, get rid of the usage of antibiotics and decide not to take them just because I am pouring the results of my investigations, convictions and firm beliefs, and especially, conclusive results: no, it won't be that easy. I repeat: with the small experiences that I mentioned lines above, I pretend to sow the doubt in you, and make you reflect and consider, and maybe decide instead of allowing the historical consequences related to diseases and their causes keep on affecting you as they have up to this moment of your life.

I deeply respect all the researchers of our past, who correctly discovered thousands of bugs that caused different diseases, and those that are yet to be found, same as the medicines and antibiotics: my profound respect for Alexander Fleming for discovering penicillin by accident (…), however, *I cannot* leave aside all that I have learned in my experience of plenty of years, especially since 1991, related to the superiority of the will against the habits or beliefs of so many decades.

What I have just mentioned in the lines of the preceding paragraph took much more relevance, like when I read Dr. Bruce Lipton's "The Biology of Belief", where he states, based on his own investigations, that:

> *"Thoughts are more powerful than diseases".*

And that:

> *"Thoughts are more powerful than any medicine".*

This very nice doctor also created the Epigenetics, which is the branch of the medicine that states with proofs and extraordinary results that genes DO NOT determine life or its quality for us, but the contrary: we are capable of modifying genetic patterns that have established that *if we carry the dominant gene* of diabetes, at some point of our lives we will become diabetic. My buddy Bruce states that we are all definitely capable of modifying this and living a life designed based on our decisions and convictions, and not based in what is now known as dominant hereditary factors.

If you think about the history of medicine, you will notice that everything, absolutely everything has been based on our fragility before the bugs (I am referring to any lousy creature, nearly invisible or not, whether it is called bacteria, virus, rickettsia, amoeba, louse, bedbug, tick or black beetle) that exist, which we live with every day. The lives of plenty of people changed when they saw Discovery Health's documentary that was dedicated to record the outrages and adventures of the mites. Before that, the stupid mites were absolutely invisible or insignificant! Now they are cause of psychosis in thousands of people and of generous businesses that swear to get rid of them.

Before, long before, any of this was real. Only the power of the human being to fight any imbalance in his body or mind and the doctors or witchdoctors or shamans of any social group were the ones to wake up the healer that we all have inside us and that way we could fight any "disease"!

Before, there were not so many Caesarean births, so many surgeries and we, descendants of those who did not know them are alive! The needed question is, and how did they survive? How did we survive?

As there are more medical breakthroughs and more scientific discoveries, more and more medicines are produced, and more and more diseases are born. Bacteria develop tolerance to the antibiotics and more "last generation" medicines appear, of course, that supposedly kick the resistant bacteria's butts, and do the same to the patient's wallet, not to mention the intestinal flora. The answers that emerge to the questions of the family or the friends after the patient has been cured "thanks" to the action of that new and very expensive antibiotic are based on their gratitude to the doctor that prescribed it, on the now famous antibiotic, but *never* on the intervention of their own decision of overcoming this infections process, or on their faith in themselves! With the latter, I want to say that we trust in *external* factors, again, and not in our healing ability, fundamental component that has been there even before our birth.

We have given so much power with the passing of history to the medicines that we have created the biggest industry that exists nowadays: the pharmaceutical industry. Additionally, we have discredited the faith in our internal healer so much, that divine bit we all have, that we are unprotected, fragile, vulnerable in front of the presence of a filthy society of bacteria nourished by publicity and the industry of the dependence: if you don't take this antibiotic you will be kick the bucket... well, that point is very well understood.

I ask myself every day, what would happen if the resources that are used to reinforce all those ideas of the powerful last gen medicine, or the new strain of virus ending with the population of certain place of our home planet, were used to investigate, discover and regain the faith and confidence in the natural healing elements, which we are born with? It would be fabulous, but this will NOT happen. Billions of dollars, euros, pesos and pounds are invested in keeping us in the idea of us requiring factors external to ourselves to *heal* what ails us.

But, what if we start trusting in that by having the will, thoughts, choices and convictions AND correct nourishment we will be able not only to heal ourselves, but avoid any ailment?

This could naturally be subject of plenty of controversy. I invite you to do an experiment when you have the *suspicion or belief* that you are going to get the flu.

Throw yourself at the bed. Get rid of anything that causes you any kind of discomfort. Get yourself comfortable and dedicate the first 5 minutes to controlling your breathing, inhaling in a rhythm you establish, and exhaling in the same way. After a while of you being who makes breathing a conscious and voluntary function, the time will come when you will most probably start feeling like "floating" or maybe you could experience a light dizziness; most probably you will stop feeling that you are on a bed, or even laying… in that precise moment, *visualize* all of your body, from your feet to your head, slowly, little by little, sending an order of resting and obeying to each one of your organs, and even each cell… issue an order to each one of the elements that form your body to harmonize and flow according to your orders. Next, direct your gaze, your will, your power to the organ that you consider to be on the verge of being affected… now issue an order to it… order it to harmonize with the rest of the components of your body and for it to distance from any malaise, for it to understand that it is a component of a marvelous element of the Creation, and that by no reason it should be victim of any external factor that could affect the wellbeing you enjoy… send in that moment every positive message, filled with energy, that you know and you consider powerful enough for that ailment to disappear immediately.

Continue for as long as you consider necessary to revitalize yourself and revitalize that part of your body that was about to be affected, until slowly and little by little you return to the moment and place you started this exercise, but not before saying to yourself: "I will wake up in a perfect state of physical health, with exquisite harmony and wellbeing in each one of the components of my body, in an incomparable wellbeing and tranquility..."

Your health is NOT established by what science says and the doctors mention, but in what YOU decide, decree and state from the present moment; from the moment you firmly believe and accept that in no way a miserable bug will come to affect your quality of life, as you are no favorable field for any "disease" to affect you, in any degree.

Same goes for every existing ailment, and such is the case when somebody goes to the doctor for certain symptoms that start to increase and that after laboratory exams and specific studies, you come back to the doctor and listen:

– "I believe I have some bad news for you".

Just a few doctors know how to deliver bad news, and initiate with this phrase, that influences the patient in the most atrocious way. And the doctor goes on:

– "We have found a malignant tumor in your... etc., etc., etc.".

Simply put yourself in the place of this person or patient. His world changes radically. Just consider what he will suffer, his closeness to death, the things he will not get to do, and an endless list of things, all of them terrible; this is why *"the thoughts of the patient are more harmful than the real disease"*, and it is much more likely for him to die because of what he believes in than the effects of that cancer per se. Let's not forget that the negative emotions and thoughts are facilitators of imbalances and malfunctions in the body, making way to any form of diseases, a symptom that might be undetermined.

From some point of my past, I remembered this that someone did as an experiment, since it was real.

When he (let's call him Daniel), when Daniel arrived to his work, after the regular routine of waking up, taking a shower, getting dressed, rushing to have his breakfast and jump into every day's traffic stream, the first coworker to welcome him, after a brief hi, says:

– "Hey, Daniel, are you sick? You don't look so good".

Daniel responds that he is feeling good, but his next coworker also says:

– "Daniel, you look like you're having a bad day. Did you go see the doctor yet?

In that moment, Daniel wonders about the reason behind the "coincidence". Well, he sits at his desk, and when his assistant comes to scene, she says:

– "Don Daniel, before going through the day's agenda, I want to know if you want me to bring you an aspirin or some other medicine, because you look a little pale and somewhat sick..."

In that moment, Daniel gets up and walks to the bathroom, sticks his tongue out and notices it with some spots, and dry, his heart rate increases, same as his blood pressure; he loosens his tie and with big steps goes to the boss's office and asks him for permission to go see the doctor.

He OBVIOUSLY goes see the doctor, who OBVIOUSLY starts the protocol: laboratory exams-results-medicines-restrictions, etc. Another "patient" is born.

THIS is precisely what thoughts and emotions can cause.

If you think you are sick, you will be sick. If you think and state and ratify being healthy, you will also be healthy!

In what moment were human beings deprived from the ability to heal themselves?

With this book, I don't pretend to radically change the way you think regarding the relation bacteria-disease, but to sow in you the desire of going deeper into yourself and getting to know the therapeutic or healing and especially preemptive potential that exists inside you and very specially what you are feeding yourself; every cell of your body has the ability to respond to your indications or orders, to harmonize and prevent or fight any type of ailment.

I read around something that I just loved, and goes like this: *"the pharmaceutical industry does not cure: it creates customers"*.

I know you are asking yourself about the limits of your ability to achieve what I have described. The answer is, there are no limits! Even in the case of a serious wound, once you have programmed your cells to recover, to regenerate, and to go back to working in a normal way, the relief will come, its functions will again be the same and you will go back to your everyday life.

Do you know that we have the ability to regenerate our limbs, just as lizards do? If our body produced such or such disease, then it has the ability to cure it, doesn't it?

Did you know that our bodies were designed to live for more than 120 years? It's only that since we are a few months old, we negatively affect this, just as the mothers who give their children Coca-Cola in their bottles to "feed" them or calm them. Then, hundreds of factors follow, which gradually destroy the autoimmune or defense factors every human being was born with.

The Hunza, who live in the limits of China, India and Afghanistan, in a region called Gilgit-Baltistan, live as much as 120 or 130 years without diseases. Of course, the diet is vital for this to happen, and that is why we will talk about it in the next chapter.

Other factors that definitely diminish notably our auto-healing ability are stress, inadequate attitude, atmospheric contamination, lack of physical activity or exercise, smoking, alcohol in excess, lack of mental exercises, television, since everything you read, you listen and see in the news is impregnating your mind with negativism; electromagnetic waves, which are present in everything that surrounds us and even in some things we carry around, such as cellphones, tablets, etc.; I could state that technology has become one of the most powerful ways in our days to keep every member of the family uncommunicated: look at any family in a restaurant: each one with their cellphone, unconnected to the real reason of his presence, "the tightening of the family bonds". In the other hand, Internet is an infinite source of information, but definitely, most of the things we see through it are not trustworthy and reliable, and are the cause of some alterations in the behavior of millions of human beings. To prove this point, it would be enough for us to see all of the views the videos filled with violence have: internet is a school for good or for evil; unfortunately, what attracts the most attention is gore, violence, destruction, fame, druglords, human trafficking and an endless array of elements that are not positive at all.

Now it surprises me to see games in the hands of children, where the one who "kills" the most people is "rewarded" with more lives, and this happens while clearly watching the puddles of blood of the one that was killed... all of this in a little device the size of a cellphone. I remember the cartoons and comics of the 60s or 70s, where these dreadful messages of violence, terror, weapons, blood, and much, much more, did not exist. What terrified me back then was movies like King

Kong. I swear that I could not sleep imagining that its huge face would appear in the window of our room! Now kids have been "programmed" to not feel frightened of hideous creations of the most diabolical minds of the movie producers, do you agree? And I wonder if this is positive. My immediate answer is that of course it isn't! And it is not because it hurts me that my grandkids are not terrified by what we couldn't even imagine before, but because the violence, the monsters, the weapons with incredible power are part of their days, and, where is their ability to be surprised left? Their innocence? Their childhood? Their creativity? Their imagination based on love? The mentioned elements have favored the existence of kids that are more intelligent but that are "less kids".

They are also addicted to junk food and beverages that they accept more than a fruit and honey smoothie, and they therefore determine a form of diet that can last for their whole lifetime, and that diminishes their auto-healing ability.

Getting rid of the habit of drinking sodas during lunch is something much more difficult than you can imagine, and is precisely why you must think in what you give your children for them to eat and drink, and of course, you need to consume it too.

Applying what I mention in the preceding paragraph is also one of the principles of *gerontoprophylaxis,* since you are sowing in your kids the concepts of a real diet that will result immensely benefic for them and their quality of life.

I will mention some points that will be pillars for your health to remain solid during your whole life and for the alterations in the balance you keep be corrected with only a moment of meditation where your auto-healing mechanisms are activated.

Eat well: We will speak about this in the next chapter. Health and illness correspond to what you eat.

Sleep well: Love your loved ones, love everything that is alive and everything that isn't, love everything that forms part of your life and your day to day. Love your work, but above all, love yourself.

Drink well: Drinking one or two glasses of red wine is a beneficial measure for your heart, given its resveratrol contents, (it is a polyphenol that can be found in some plants. It belongs to the same family as the flavonoids and tannins, and the tannins are contained in the red wine, and have medicinal properties that reduce, mainly, the probability of suffering from cardiovascular diseases); if you drink tequila or whisky, choose a good brand, and obviously do it without excesses. Be you who takes it, and not the other way around.

No smoking: Smoking will never be a good idea. Regardless of the damages it causes in your body, especially in your lungs, the dependence or addiction factor subtracts value to your ability to decide and you are then driven by a consequence, product of that addiction. Smoking is more addictive than cocaine.

Walk well: A walk from Monday to Friday with a duration of 40 minutes, in which you harmonize with the day, the sun, the people, the animals and plants that you can greet in your way will activate your circulatory and respiratory systems and your heart. Your blood pressure and your digestion will improve, and your bones will strengthen, lowering the possibilities of osteoporosis, especially in women. You will also suffer less from constipation and in general, it will make you see the world even more beautiful than it already is. If you do this walk with somebody else, the benefits will be increased.

Learn well: Keeping your mind busy and with goals, learning something new every day, exercising it constantly with things such as learning new languages, reading a book, playing checkers, chess, sudoku, jigsaw puzzles, learning to paint, to knit, and an endless list of manual activities that will surely keep your mind alive and functional, as the mind is a muscle that requires activity and effort to solve the challenges described in this point.

Plan well: In the same measure in which you have plans and goals to follow, you will have a very powerful element to have an excellent health. The individual of any age that retires from the productive life (with the word "productive" I am not referring to producing material wealth, but to creating, generating, innovating), turns into a fragile being and maybe in plenty of cases unhappy and even invisible, since the potential of the knowledge that he has accumulated during his life will be buried along with him when he dies. This SHOULD NOT happen. Read, write a book, leave your descendants something that has more value than a handful of money and properties, and be advised: in the point that talks about *material possessions* widely described before, among the plans you choose, they need to consider spending your savings and acquiring that thing that fills you with satisfaction: a new car, the watch you always wanted, the trip of your dreams, since, and I repeat: *"If you don't fly first class, your inheritors will"*. *Consider that it is better to die chasing a goal or a dream that reaching the final moment of your existence with a "what if" in your thoughts.*

Socialize well, laugh a lot: Socializing is elemental for your health. Periodic get-togethers with your friends, speaking about whatever but illnesses, will give a lot color to those moments and to the upcoming days. Also, you will be eager for the day of next week's get-together to come to feed on those delicious moments. Laughter is an infallible remedy and also a powerful vaccine against any illness.

Pray well: Praying will never be the same as reciting, just the same as spirituality has nothing to do with religion. Praying is the most profound expression of love for you and everyone you love. When you recite, you repeat something that is indeed beautiful, but you stop comprehending its meaning when you repeat it so many times: when you *recite* it. When you pray, you open your senses and your power to communicate with your Teacher, regardless of your beliefs. After you pray, *meditate*. I have the conviction that when you pray you communicate with your Teacher, and when you meditate, **He** communicates with you. I will just leave you a subtle suggestion: make your prayer so that it does not contains petitions, but offerings: make your prayer an *offertory sheet* instead of a *petitionary sheet*. Praying is healthy, soothing and harmonizes you with the Universe.

Commitments with myself.

After several decades of my life, I found and learnt some lessons from my real teachers –the elders– and from there, I defined 5 commitments with myself that I now share with you and would love if you made them yours for yourself.

1.- Be happy. Life is not perfect, we know it, but because it isn't, it allows us to learn from the "imperfect" moments. This will definitely bring us to be students; to learn and be happy with what has been learnt. This is why I know I'm happy, sometimes with bruises caused by the falls, but they are prizes from which I learnt and grew.

2.- Learn. Learn every day from everything that happens to you, from all the people you meet, because it is marvelous. Learn to learn, but also learn to unlearn! The list of acquired knowledge during your life is an invaluable treasure you should NOT die with, and therefore, you have this next commitment:

3.- Teach or share the learnings. In the preceding point or commitment, I mention that you SHOULD NOT die with everything you have learnt during our life. Therefore, you MUST share it in any way possible. The best way to do it is through a book. That is what I do. That is *another* goal I have set.

4.- Leave this world better than it was when I found it. This is so darn hard, but if not the whole world, do it for your surroundings, for your social groups, for your country, for the world you move within every day. Push yourself to leave something that is transcendent and that makes someone smile when he remembers you. This will mark the *difference* and you will have changed this that I have called *the world*.

5.- Make love a way of life. In the deepest and most transcendent sense of the phrase, if you love yourself, if you love your couple, the members of your family, the inhabitants of your country and the whole world, you will be healthy in the widest sense of the word. If you get home, and even if you live without company (this DOES NOT mean solitude, but decision) and you yell: "I'm home" and you greet your living room, your kitchen, your bed... heavens! You are living in love for what you are and surrounds you; if you are with your family and you kiss every one of its members, and you let them know how important they are for you, you are fulfilling this commitment with yourself... and even more.

As I mentioned, I hope you make these commitments yours for yourself, and –back to health– you will be healthy in every moment.

I perceive in this moment that I have not yet shared and invited you to reflect. It is, according to what I think, the "formula" to solve every problem in the world, and it is the G.A.W.F.F.A.L.C. formula.

G.: Gratitude. Give thanks daily to your Teacher, your beliefs or the Universe of what you are, what you have, what you receive, since it is no more and no less of what you deserve, what you aspire, dream and fight to obtain. Instead of requesting, thank, and the rest will come in the precise moment, when you require it and when you need it for your growth.

A.: Acceptance. This is the first big step towards solving everything that upsets or hurts you, whether it is health, financial, familiar, legal or any other kind of problem. When accepting, you show others and yourself the ability you have to face anything you have to solve. Without acceptance, nothing can be solved, since you are establishing a wall between reality and your position. This could be interpreted as denial. Accept that there is something worrying you and take steps to solve it, whatever it may be.

W.: Work. With this, I don't pretend to describe what is represented by going every day to an office or to a place where you execute a task you are paid a certain amount of money for. No! What I mean is establishing goals and purposes to keep on being creative, current, emphasizing your vocation and dreams more than you did when you only worked for the financial relief and solution to the basic living and feeding needs it represented. By work, I pretend to emphasize the need we have of creating, of establishing goals, of dreaming and chasing those dreams... those friends. It is essential to make this world a better place.

F.: Faith. It is said that faith can do it all. Faith in yourself will let you achieve anything, *anything* you set your mind to: limits are established by yourself. Here is a quick advice: DO NOT establish any limit: only rhythm and time.

F.: Forgiveness. Wow! And Oops! Forgiving yourself and forgiving frees you from the heaviest load your shoulders can bear. First of all, we blame God or our Teacher when things are not or do not turn out how we wanted them to or how we asked them to. This is the moment to forgive Him, as our life project is already established long before we were born, and what happens is no more and no less than a plan for our learning and growth, despite the hard hits we receive throughout our life. It is not fair either to consider ourselves stupid, simply because a guy called Sergio promised the moon and the stars, and we blindly trusted. Darned Sergio (name anyone) is only a teacher and we are pupils; we candidly call our trust "faith" or "innocence". Despicable Sergio considers it stupidity and takes advantage of us. Each one of us tries to do what each considers "fair", according to the way we think and act, but if by doing so we hurt someone, it is NOT our "fault": it is just that we act by own principles. This is why expressing "I forgive you, darned Sergio, for making me believe something that harmed me", will set us free and we will then be able to use it as a lesson. Forgive God or your Teacher, scumbag Sergio, your ex-wife, who kept all the savings you had placed in a foreign bank, the guy who kicked your butt in a bar fight, the dog who pissed on your shoes in one of the worst days of your life or the guy that sold you those delicious tacos that caused you the most liquid of your diarrheas the next day: nobody pretends to insult you: we are all pursuing what we think is fair, or our reasons; nobody kicks your butt to hurt you: he is only doing what he thinks is right: nobody offends you: it is only you who accepts a phrase as "offense", since you also look for elements to "offend" the one who "offended" you. Forgive, but above all, forgive yourself.

A.: Attitude. Yes: attitude achieves everything or loses everything. When you value the teachings of a "failure" or a "fall" and you understand it as a lesson and learning, everything that happens will be positive, valuable and will make you grow: *positive attitude*. If from that fall you familiarize with the ground, with the dust on it, with everything that is stepped on and disregarded by the rest of the people, you will never get on your feet: *negative attitude*. Decide and define your attitude right now.

L.: Love. I have already mentioned this in several occasions: love yourself: love everything that lives and everything that does not live but forms part of your world; love your computer, every object that surrounds you and in any moment you will see that you have answer of each one of them, as by loving you flood of power and energy all that forms part of your choices and not of the *consequences*.

C.: Compassion. Compassion does NOT have anything to do with pity. Pity could even be offensive. Compassion is placing yourself in the life, in the shoes of another human being to perceive his way of living to understand him and then to help him. NOT with spare change, but with support and motivation... listening to him. Who asks for spare change is a manipulator; who asks for support is an open being waiting for your *compassion* to give him the "push" he needs to move on and keep on going.

Health is NOT a git from God, that in spite of every excess you will keep. Health is not only the result of taking medicines and multivitamins either, or not smoking or not drinking alcohol. Health is not going to the doctor when you feel ill, or getting up early and running 5 kilometers every day: it is much more than this: it is all of the above together with what I have mentioned in all of the preceding pages, and especially harmonizing yourself with each cell in your body, speaking to them and making them know that they are part of a universe of well-being and harmony, which together will fill your life with quality and dignity, until the last moment, meaning especially in the last moment.

ALTERNATIVE MEDICINES

If we are speaking so up front about the side effects of the allopathic medicines, I know that in this moment you are asking yourself what "remedies" should be the ones you should be taking to heal when some disease appears in your body, besides the attitude and every point and suggestion I have just mentioned. This is the moment to tell you some of the alternatives that exists to heal you once a process called "disease" is installed in your body.

I must state and confirm at all costs a convincing fact: despite all of your positive attitude, a good diet, a healthy environment and if possible, healthy, it will always be possible for a process that alters your health to be installed. By saying this, I don't mean to tell you that you *necessarily* have to go to the allopath to ask for all that process I have mentioned repeatedly. My question is: where are all the medicines the "patients" take obtained from? From plants! And then, why the hell don't we give our so-called patients those herbs in teas, ointments, capsules, or even better: along with the food, as a preventive component?

As I mentioned before, the best medicine is the preventive medicine, and therefore, before speaking about herbalism or other alternatives that lead to health, I will talk to you a little bit about the benefits that would provide to our health if we took along with our daily meals certain elements that definitely and convincingly will help you keep healthy all the time.

It does not matter if you are a vegetarian, lacto-ovo-vegetarian, vegan, carnivore, or any other nutritional alternative that exists. I only want to mention that if you add to your meals some of the following, you could have excellent health: curcuma, black pepper and ginger, as well as seeds of chia, pumpkin, hemp (it contains the 10 amino acids), pomegranate, flax, apricot (the seed that the apricot has inside it –and you may have to take it out with a hammer– a little almond that contains B17 vitamin, one of the most powerful anticarcinogenic agent that exists. Note: This little almond is toxic when more than one a day is taken, so don't take more. One a day would even help in the healing process of some kinds of cancer), sunflower, sesame, cumin and grape.

Still on the same food train of thought, if you cook with coconut oil, you will be "getting yourself vaccinated" against plenty, plenty of the chronic degenerative diseases that are "in stile", your "bad" cholesterol will be lowered, your mental and physical condition will improve, your blood pressure will be more stable and even controlled, you WILL NOT gain weight, and plenty of things more; another alternatives are avocado oil, grape seed oil, nut oil, sesame oil, etc. I would NOT recommend soy oil, because after some weeks of eating it, you will be making your liver suffer, since it does not have the ability to handle that kind of oil adequately. Olive oil is excellent for salads, as long as it is cold-pressed, virgin or extra virgin. It is not the best option for cooking, because, at relatively high temperatures, it oxidizes and loses its positive virtues, and is left as any other oil in the market.

Ok. We are talking about alternative medicines. I want, in a very convincing way, to mention that asthma is NOT curable with allopathic medicine, no. Only the symptoms are cared for, but medicines such as homeopathic, ayurvedic, herbal, traditional Chinese, Indian, Cuban, etc., DO cure it. Therefore, I would very much advise you to investigate a little bit more on Pita, Kappa and Vata of ayurvedic medicine, and consider that what you have beside your thoughts and positive attitude could help you improve your quality of life.

Presently, I am preparing many protocols to attend diseases of every kind, from cancer to demential ailments, in which I include antioxidants, agonists (I will elaborate later on the application of stem cells, which I consider to be the medicine of the future, TODAY), regenerative medicine and even the medicinal part of the marihuana called cannabidiol or CBD, which has been tremendously helping me in the control of neurological and demential problems, along with glutathione. As an example, I can tell you that there was a child that had epileptic seizures as often as 20 a day, and I started treating him with drops of CBD. His crises went down to 2 or 3 per month.

Along with these protocols, I am including Ayurvedic Medicine, and in the upcoming weeks I will be able to offer preventive and even healing "packages" for plenty of those diseases with strange, unpronounceable names, and even impossible to care for or cure with the medicine we usually use in west. One of my dreams is to call for a one week get-away so that you can spend this time in a very beautiful and adequate place for the purpose, receiving a diet that has been specifically designed for your health situation or needs to improve the quality of your present and close-future life, with the most precise activities, and sow in you a new image that makes you do a complete change in your life. Please get informed on the achievements I have reached in the moment you are reading this book.

If you are suffering from some chronic degenerative disease, I can offer an orientation through email to you, with the purpose of improving your quality of life in every sense.

Alternative medicines offer an unimaginable quantity of real solutions to plenty of diseases. As I have already mentioned, the purpose of this book is not to establish dietary patterns, or recipes to cure or care for the thousands of ailments that exist nowadays, but to sow in you the inquisitiveness to know more of your body, and especially, the effect that causes in it and its every organ the emotions, the thoughts and the bad habits when eating, and all of the aforementioned, simply based in habits that go from generation to generation, and that have left behind what really worked in the cultures that existed centuries ago. I simply wonder how we would have survived if shamans, witch doctors or healers in the ancient cultures of the whole world would not have existed.

In certain periods of my life, I have lived in almost desertic or uninhabited environments, and their health problems were looked after by their witch doctors; the births by the midwives, who did not practice Caesarean sections, and everything was solved properly. I witnessed curations of rattlesnake bites several times, people that where injured with machetes during fights; can you imagine the amount of blood they lost, as well as the seriousness of their injuries? And they where taken care of by their doctor, who gave them potions prepared with the herbs they collected in the field, placed poultices in the wounds and then celebrated some sort of ceremony with religious contents, and they healed!

I once met a foreign doctor from the United States that practiced the Coyote Medicine, who through meditation took you to meet your "coyote guide", which is found –according to him– within all of us and when invoked, pointed out the ailment, its origin and its cure. In many occasions, he used ayahuasca and in some others, peyote.

How did your grandma or great-grandma cured a cold and even bronchitis? She DID NOT treat fever with medicines, but with teas, chicken broth, a cotton with alcohol in your navel, Vick's VapoRub rubbed in neck, chest, back and soles of your feet. Two days in bed and you're good to go! Now, if you are not prescribed antibiotics, you feel that your treatment is not complete.

I have had the chance to meet healers that with certain manipulations in the affected part of the bodies, save many people from surgeries; in Guadalajara, the "carbonero" was very famous. He was a traditional healer that treated you for any problem in joints and bones; there is (I hope he still lives) a herbalist in San Luis Soyatlan, Jalisco, who sees dozens of people every day with different ailments and is right in 75 to 80% of the cases.

Give yourself the opportunity of reading about the benefits of the Mexican herbal medicine, the traditional medicine of our Mexico, the traditional Chinese medicine, the Ayurvedic and the Cuban medicine, and you will see that there are plenty of things that we have been losing because "science" has been displacing them with its modernity, technology and even the ego of plenty of doctors who in a moment of their lives feel like demigods or like someone with the power to "heal" every "disease".

I mention the marvels of the humble sodium bicarbonate in a very precise and insistent way, which can even cure cancers; the well-directed meditation, the diets that contain substances that avoid any growth of malignant cells; therefore, do not let this fall on deaf ears.

In my daily practice, I now use them and the complementary medicine is, plenty of times, allopathic! I often feel that the only thing I haven't tried is dancing around the patient with a rattle, emitting weird sounds from the bottom of my lungs to achieve progress faster.

A point I wish to highlight as a rebel and "breaker of paradigms" in my decision of applying Stem Cells as part of the regenerative medicine I practice and recommend; they are certainly not the panacea, but in the time I have been using them, I have seen great results. In many diseases of immunologic origin, I use them with other stimulants of the immunologic system: certain spices I recommend you to add to your diet, very powerful anti-oxidants, and potentiating their ability with a fabulous agonist: glutathione. Do not hesitate in getting in touch with me so that I can give you all of the information and support you require in cases where the allopathic medicine says that "there is no remedy".

Now, some tips:

Cancerous cells cannot live with oxygen nor in an alkaline environment. Therefore, we could avoid and even heal problems the size of cancers with completely negative allopathic diagnosis. Now, not everything is cancer, but problems that aggravate with the passing of the years, bad nutrition and lack of adequate exercise and positive attitude, however, I offer some suggestions that will help improve what you live every day and what you will live in the near future.

Water. Yes, water is essential for the life of every living being; right now, we are talking about your life and how to live it with quality. I suggest the following "formula" to drink water in the best of conditions and benefits.

1 liter of water.

4 to 5 slices of lemon, orange, lime, and cucumber, all with their skin and properly washed and dried. Washing all the components with white vinegar and water is an excellent idea.

1 heaping tablespoon of grated ginger, perfectly clean.

1 tablespoon of ground linseed.

2 tablespoons of sodium bicarbonate.

2 tablespoons of chia seed.

Half a teaspoon of ground turmeric (you can find it in grocery stores or in spice stores)... This is not publicity: I am just looking to make it easier for you to find the components.

7-10 mint leaves.

Prepare this the night before and consume it the next day. If you wish to sweeten it, do it with honey, never with white or brown sugar, or with artificial sweetener. Maybe leaves or natural Stevia powder: nothing else.

Another tip:

If before starting with your activities in the morning, you prepare half a cup of warm water with half a teaspoon of sodium bicarbonate and some drops of lemon, leaving a slice of the same lemon with its skin to rest in the mixture inside your cup for a minute, and you take it half an hour before your breakfast and at the end of your day, you will see incredible benefits in the quality of your day to day life.

Another tip:

Memory problems? Drink turmeric tea every day, sweetened with honey; incredible results when you do it for weeks. Within those protocols I have just mentioned, I will be able to offer one that contains anti-oxidants and an element used in the ayurvedic medicine to improve memory and cognitive functions.

More tips:

Do you wish to detox? Prepare a shake based in raw beet and no peel, two green apples, two sticks of celery and two or three radishes (use the small and round ones). Put everything in the blender, add water and a pinch of ground black pepper, some grains of sea salt or Himalaya salt, and drink it during three consecutive mornings... when you go to the toilet all sorts of things will come out!

Another one:

In winter, many old aged die from pneumonia, and that is the origin of a phrase I don't like that much that says "enero y febrero, desviejadero" in Spanish, which means that January and February are the months when more old aged people die, and it is very true, precisely because of those respiratory problems I was mentioning. Around 20 years ago, I started recommending the following to the elderlies I attend: 1 monthly vial of Benzathine penicilllin1'200,000 (heads up, NOT the combined one, but the one that says 1'200'000 U.I.) units from October to March; vitamin C, 2 grams daily during this same period or six weeks, then rest two weeks, and then 6 weeks again, Echinacea in syrup or drops, and administer according to the instructions in the bottle, as it varies according to the laboratory that fabricates it, ginger and cinnamon tea, sweetened with honey every day, and vitamins A and D. There are some presentations in vials that are edible, and do not have to be injected.

More?

Woman: if you have memory issues, you went to the doctor and mentioned something related to problems with your brain, I would suggest that you go to a laboratory and get a second stream urine exam. Ask for more information in the laboratory of your choice. If you present a urinary infection, your memory is surely being affected; it would greatly help if you acidified your urine or take an antiseptic so that this is modified and even cured.

Alzheimer? I will tell you what I recommend: tea or capsules of Mexican thistle, a powerful anti-oxidant. Another powerful agonist, the glutathione, alkaline diet, mental exercises, physical activity, stem cells, CBD, vitamin D3, 5,000 units daily and vitamin K2. For any reason would I prescribe the things that the pharmaceutical industry "says" that works, This and other protocols for the attention of the so-called "dementia" problems can be found in the work I spoke to you about.

Flu? Take ginger and cinnamon tea sweetened with honey and a Japanese garlic every day. Stay in bead for at least 24 hours and you will see the changes. If you rub in your chest and the soles of your feet slices of red onion seared in the hotplate, and you even place it in your soles under a "wrapping" of the plastic wrap a lot of food is wrapped in, the next morning you will notice exquisite changes.

For the endogen depression, which is the one that presents when you don't know what is causing it, take a pearl of vitamin D3 of 5,000 units with a handful of cashews with NO salt once a day. The best anti-depressant is one that we produce and that is called tryptophan, and with the passing of the years, we produce it in less quantity. With this combination, the production of this amino acid is activated and progressively, the depression starts to disappear.

The joints that are affected and painful, caused by the excess of our youth are greatly relieved with magnesium chloride: boil 30 grams in a liter o water and to stir it use a wooden spoon. Once it is ready, let it cool down, place it in a jar of glass and save it. Take one to two tablespoons a day. It has a discreet laxative effect. I wouldn't advise you to take it if you have renal insufficiency or ulcerative colitis. Besides, it has plenty of positive effects to keep you with an excellent health.

The wounds in the skin and superficial muscles can be relieved with a solution of colloidal silver. You can find it in stores that sell natural products, and according to the laboratory that produces it, is the way to use it. Ask for orientation to the pharmacist that sells it.

Another wonder is garlic. With only one clove of garlic you take a day or with every meal, you will obtain benefits such as improving the cognitive functions of the brain and lowering the "bad" cholesterol. It is considered a natural antibiotic, helps control hypertension, frees you from heavy metals and has other favorable effects.

Onion cannot be left behind. It collaborates in maintaining the glucose levels stable in the diabetic, has a discreet laxative effect because of the fiber it contains, is a good diuretic, has a bactericide effect, favors the purification of the blood, as well as many other virtues. In cases of flu, the chicken broth with plenty of onion helps for a faster healing.

If there is always lemonade in your refrigerator, and it has some slices of lemon with its skin, it is very recommendable to avoid minor infectious diseases, and even some mayor. Use only honey to sweeten it.

THIRD PART

NUTRITION

When I finished studying, the *need* to know about very essential points for the exercising of the medical profession crossed my mind: nutrition, humility, humanism, the ability to give bad news and the ability to accept that we can make mistakes.

Thanks to the smiles of gratitude of my patients –my real teachers–, I started to learn little by little about the exercise of humility, humanism, I learned to give bad news in a more subtle and human way, different; it was very hard to accept that I made mistakes and even more recognizing it in front of the patient, but the hardest part was to understand that the elemental factor for a body of any human being to function as close to perfection as possible is based on *nutrition*, and NOT in the medicines he takes.

I will mention again the answer I gave to that patient that came out of my medical dispensary, asking if the medicine (or treatment) needed to include certain diet, and thinking fast, I only told her not to take coffee or black sodas, or pork meat, or fat, or spices, etc. All of the above just came out of my mind because I remembered what one of my teachers had said to his patient in a similar situation.

Now I realize that establishing a list of restrictions is part of the protocol that the medical consultation *demands*, besides of the prescription with two or more medicines. Then, this pops into my mind:

But, what if instead of that list of restrictions and medicines, the patient was prescribed a series of combinations of fruits, vegetables, seeds, cereals and beverages?

What if instead of going to the doctor to cure an ailment that has already presented, you do so for him to *prevent* it?

Do we: nourish or eat? Is fat in food really bad and causes an increase in cholesterol? Do you only eat the egg white because you think that the yolk is harmful? There would be plenty of questions coming up on so many myths, beliefs, and of course, realities in the field of nutrition. As doctors, I feel that we must have enough knowledge to adequately advise our patients regarding what is the most convenient to eat or to avoid; I understand that it is easier to throw a series of restrictions instead of giving advises; as people, I also feel we must also be informed to request, wait or demand that our doctor includes in his prescription a series of suggestions related to the nutriments that will complement the indicated treatment, and even prevent from worse ailments.

Talking about nutrition is really quite a maze. I noticed this when in that Congress of Integrative Medicine I mentioned before, simultaneously, or maybe with a one hour difference, the benefits of vegetarianism were being addressed, while in the room across, the speaker was saying that we had to drink milk and eat meat and eggs, and in another room, they were saying that we should not eat milk OR meat OR eggs, and in another, that we should eat eggs, milk and vegetables... now there are some other names, such as "vegan" diet, and if it was not enough, the "paleodiet". Holy names and confusions!

My purpose with this book is giving you an orientation that might be a little shallow so that you sharpen your innate senses to eat better and healthier with certain direction based in the each's own experiences. I am totally sure that you will find that some of the things I suggested are being strongly fought by other doctors, and even nutritionists. My knowledge in the field of nutrition is limited, however, they it has been directed towards the *prevention* of the "diseases that affect the old aged", naturally based in *prevention*, and if we speak about preventive medicine, it is mandatory to speak about the best nutrition possible from a very early age, in such a way that we are preventing through the things we eat, and as consequence, we get an old age with a better quality. It is very clear to me that there are ailments or diseases that present after many years of eating according to the customs, habits, publicity, culture, etc., without paying attention to the benefits or problems that this may cause.

Such is the case of fat.

Fat.- Concentrated sources of energy. 30% of our daily nutrition should be this. The fat that comes from fish and vegetable sources is the best kind. Fat can be saturated or non-saturated (unsaturated). This last one is liquid at room temperature; the saturated is solid and comes from animal sources and produces the food for "bad" cholesterol.

The non-saturated fat is divided into two kinds: the monounsaturated, contained in a high concentration in olive oil, and the polyunsaturated, which is present in the corn (maize), saffron, sunflower and soybean oil. These are NOT convenient for cooking, as they do not resist high temperatures and are easily oxidized, losing the benefits of the Omega 3 they contain. Particularly, soybean oil is not easily manageable by our liver after a while of consuming it. I don't recommend milk, soymilk or soybean oil. These Omega 3 are also contained in salmon, mackerel and sardine. Amazingly, the chia seed possess 5 times more Omega 5 than salmon! Therefore, if every night you prepare a liter of lemonade with two tablespoons of chia seeds and you take it during the following day, once the chia seed has swollen, you will have a magnificent result. I would not advise you to ingest dry chia. It is a proven fact that a daily gram of Omega 3 lowers 25% the risk of a heart attack in people that has suffered from some kind of cardiopathy.

Omega 3 is a polyunsaturated fat that lowers the "bad" or low-density cholesterol, and increases the high density, or "good" cholesterol.

Cook with coconut oil and you will find extraordinary benefits in your health. Other options are avocado, peanut (groundnut), walnut, grape (which are a little bit pricy, but with a good justification) and olive oil, but this last one does not resist high temperatures. I would rather use it or recommend it for salads. It has to be cold-pressed, organic, virgin or extra virgin.

I want to point out something VERY important: fat is NOT the direct cause of the increase in bad cholesterol or triglycerides, but the carbohydrates, when combined with the saturated or trans fat, which also favor obesity.

I will make some comments on cholesterol. It is a steroid lipid (not exactly a kind of fat) essential for the body. It forms the base of the production of the vitamin D (even those who take supplements get around 90% of their vitamin D from the skin) of hormones, steroids, myelin and tallow.

Cholesterol is not bad for the body; in fact, it is essential for life, for the functioning of the neurons and plenty of functions of the whole body.

There are two kinds of cholesterol: one known as "good", and the other one known as "bad" cholesterol. As a matter of fact, it is not really "bad", but the lipoproteins that form it, but let's not get into so many names and blabber.

Triglycerides are really harmful and are associated with diabetes and cardiac diseases. Some factors that increase this substance in the organism are consumption of simple carbohydrates, sedentarism, consumption of alcohol, overweight, and smoking.

We find in the body high concentrations of cholesterol in the liver, which in fact produces it, in the vesicle, in the nervous system, and in the skin.

The liver uses it to produce steroid hormones, such as sexual hormones, aldosterone and cortisol. As you can see, there is nothing wrong with it, and plenty of indispensable.

Egg, cholesterol and other myths.- There are other running myths regarding the relation of egg and cholesterol. They say that eggs have plenty of cholesterol. Yes, there is cholesterol in eggs, but our body produces and contains more than what the innocent egg could provide; they say that you should only eat the egg whites, and only one or two a week, etc., etc., but truth is that egg is an excellent food that contains folic acid, vitamin B12, riboflavin, vitamin D, and above all, lutein. Lutein is very useful to help treat macular degeneration. One or maybe two eggs a day would be fantastic to help keep an adequate nutrition at any age. If your low-density cholesterol, or "bad" is very high, lower the consumption of egg, but to dramatically lower your levels of this cholesterol, as well as those of triglycerides, lower your consumption of sugar.

Something that is really harmful in your daily diet are fried chips, since you combine starch, trans fat and mineral salt... same happens with breaded and fried food, such as those that are sold in international food chains.

The five whites.- You should definitely eliminate the five whites from your daily diet. The five whites are: refined sugar, especially, but also the brown sugar, refined flour, mineral salt (you can change to sea salt if needed, as it does not retain liquids or increases the blood pressure, as it is said, and Himalaya salt is even better), white rice and cow's milk. Yes! Cow's milk! It contains casein in very high quantities.

Casein represents 84% of the dairy proteins and is one of the components of the cow's milk that causes the most allergies along with the a-Lactalbumin and b-Lactoglobulin. Cow's milk contains 300% more casein than breast milk, and that is why it is implicated in plenty of allergic processes.

Casein is a rough, dense and sticky that tends to accumulate in the respiratory and digestive systems, and it is very hard to eliminate through the organism. The allergic symptoms that the casein produces tend to be in a gastric level and very similar to those caused by lactose intolerance. That is why those two pathologies often get confused.

In the respiratory level, casein is guilty for the excess of mucus that many people that drink cow's milk suffer from, since it can be as serious as obstructing the respiratory airways. It has been demonstrated that children that present recurrent respiratory episodes due to excess of mucus get better if the casein is taken away from their diet.

It is also blamed for many forms of cancer.

I have just "pirated" from my buddy "Dr. John F. Unruh, from the Neurological Rehabilitation International Consultants the following:

1.- Milk reduces iron in small children. This is why in 1993, the American Academy of Pediatrics of the United States published an official statement expressing that in their opinion, any child should take animal milk before they are at least 18 months old. Also, it contributes in the lack of essential fatty acids and Vitamin E.

2.- The cow's milk stimulates the body to produce mucus in the lungs. This is why when you suffer from a flu very often, the doctor should recommend not to drink cow's milk.

3.- Milk is filled with bacteria. Therefore, it is an excellent vehicle to make bacteria grow in your body. That is why children that don't drink milk or dairy products that come from animals don't get sick so often and suffer from less dental cavities and less ear infections. The pasteurization used by the milk industry usually takes 15 seconds. However, for the bad bacteria of the milk to become inactive, the pasteurization process be done during at least 15 minutes.

4.- Casein is a protein that is present in milk and is used to manufacture glue. In most of the children, it causes swelling of the soft tissues. These soft tissues can be found most commonly in the throat, nasal cavities and paranasal sinuses. When these are swollen, there can be difficulties to breathe.

5.- Drinking and consuming dairy products is associated with many diseases such as diabetes, multiple sclerosis, heart diseases, Crohn's disease, irritable bowel syndrome (commonly known as "colitis") and even cataracts.

6.- Milk contains abnormal quantities of antibiotics, since the farmers inject them to the cows to avoid them from stopping the production of milk because of diseases in their udders. These kinds of diseases are common in the herds that produce dairy. These abnormal quantities of antibiotics contribute to the bacteria becoming more resistant to them, causing them to be harder to combat when we are talking about more serious diseases.

7.- Dairy and its derivatives contain excessive amounts of female hormones. 80% of cows are pregnant while they are used to produce milk, which naturally elevates the levels of these hormones. Besides, the farmers inject the cows with synthetic hormones to increase the production of milk. These high level of female hormones in the diet chain has been linked with health problems all around the world. They are also associated with precocious puberty.

8.- Milk contains large quantities of saturated or "bad" fat, which, when combined with carbohydrates, favor the blockage of arteries (atheromatosis), even in young people.

9.- Sugar in milk (lactose) is very hard to digest, since when a person reaches the age of 2, the intestines fabricate less lactase, an enzyme that is necessary for the absorption and the digestion of the lactose. This decrease in the production of lactase in humans happens when the ingestion of breast milk is not needed for the growth. When we consume milk or dairy products, it is very likely for the lactose to be fermented in the intestines, causing digestive problems such as swelling, gas and other serious difficulties.

10.- Milk contains a perfect combination of minerals that are designed to help mature the digestive system of the animal's offspring. This digestive system will allow them to correctly digest the nutrients of the grass and herbs. The cows have a stomach that is configured by four chambers, and they regurgitate, chew and swallow their food many times before digesting it. They have a digestive system that is very different from ours, and therefore have different needs. When we consume milk, we are ingesting the minerals and chemicals the cows need in their system, and since our diets are different, those chemicals and minerals disrupt our digestion and affects the absorption of the nutrients that are present in our diets.

11.- Milk occupies a high spot in the list of the products that cause allergies and sensibilities.

12.- Handicapped kids that suffer from neurological problems such as autism, Down's syndrome, learning disabilities and cerebral lesions are especially vulnerable to dairy. Certain proteins that are present in animal milk, such as casein, apparently irritate the nervous system of the humans, causing these neurological problems to aggravate in children. This is why, if milk or dairy is not ingested, the rehabilitation programs produce better results than the ones observed in children who ingest this type of food.

13.- Some studies have proved that consuming the hormones, cholesterol and fat found in animal milk causes a person to be more likely to develop acne and wrinkles in their skin.

14.- People that have Asian, African, Hispanic or southern Europe ascendance are especially vulnerable to the problems associated with the consumption of milk. This explains why most of the countries in the world do not consume milk.

15.- Milk is one of the substances that contain the most dioxins. Contrary to the common belief, dioxins in the milk and cheese are ten times more likely to cause cancer. During the summer of 1999, the milk industry in Brussels closed for a month because the milk contained 100 times more of the recommended levels of dioxin.

16.- Milk contains animal blood.

17.- Milk contains pus. The rules of United States Department of Health and Human Services and the Food and Drug Administration stipulate that milk is abnormal and should not be ingested if it contains more than 200,000 dead white cells by milliliter. In 2001, milk that was produced in 48 states of the United States was examined to determine if it fulfilled the rules of the FDA. Every state exceeded the allowed limits.

18.- Milk is associated with the prostate cancer in men. Risks increase by 30% if two to three portions by day are consumed. Women that take dairy products increase their risk of contracting ovary cancer by up to 66%.

19.- Consumption of milk and cheese is associated with asthma. When humans consume the casein protein contained in milk, they produce histamine and then mucus. If the bronchi are filled with this substance, difficulty to breathe is presented.

20.- Kids that drink plenty of milk and consume plenty of cheese are often low on zinc.

21.- Milk is high in "bad" cholesterol, which produces heart diseases.

22.- The stories associated with calcium and milk consumption are mostly myths created by the milk industry, who in their publicity campaigns state that cow's milk contains great quantities of calcium. Strategically, they also say that we need calcium. These two statements are both true, however, they do not mention that milk consumption gives us this calcium, since this is not the way it happens. Calcium in milk combines with other minerals that exist in excessive quantities in animal milk, forming a molecule that is most of the time very large to be absorbed by the human intestine. In areas of the world where milk is not consumed, the diseases associated with the lack of calcium are almost non-existent. Osteoporosis and atherosclerosis are very rare in cultures where consumption of milk is limited.

23.- The regulation of the presence of the vitamin D in milk is very defective. Recently, it was found that in 42 samples, only 12% contained the promised quantity of vitamin D. Also, 10 samples of baby formula were studied. 7 of them contained twice as much of the vitamin D that was announced. One of them even had 4 times as much.

24.- Drinking milk could contribute to the bone fractures. In a study of 78,000 women done throughout a period of 12 years, milk did not reduce the risk of fractures. In fact, women that drank milk three times a day had more fractures that those who rarely had it, and this is caused because bones become harder, and thus more fragile, just as crystal.

25.- Another important factor is cholesterol and the risk of cardiac and circulatory diseases. 8 ounces of milk equal 14 pieces of bacon. A glass of milk equals 35mg of cholesterol. 4 pieces of bacon equal 30mg of cholesterol.

26.- Other of the effects that are associated with the consumption of animal milk include diarrhea and constipation, especially in young people.

Did I discourage you enough?

At this point I should mention other options different than cow's milk, such as coconut milk, almond milk, oatmeal milk and even rice milk, although this last one is not advisable for diabetics and needs to be enriched with vitamins and minerals, as contents are very low in it. The described beverages, besides of fulfilling the nutritional requirements, provide additional benefits to improve your health, especially pistachio milk.

Pistachio milk is constituted as an excellent beverage that is healthy for the heart, thanks to the different healthy fat it contains, as it is rich in monounsaturated fat and oleic acid.

It is also rich in anti-oxidant nutrients such as carotenes and phytosterols, which translates into not only anti-oxidant, but anticarcinogen and rejuvenating benefits. It is an interesting milk, not only as an alternative to cow's milk, but also as traditional remedy in the case of high cholesterol and triglycerides. It also helps when increasing defenses thanks to its very high contents of vegetal proteins, where arginine stands out.

I am not very fond of soy milk, since after a short period of consuming it, it inhibits the absorption of nutrients and alters the correct functioning of the hormones: our liver does not feel comfortable metabolizing it. In fact, its boom happened thanks to publicity, just the same as many other products.

Proteins.- In these past years, many years in fact, adequate nutrition has boomed around the world, given the convincing knowledge of the fact that it is better to prevent than to heal. Even though there are many discrepancies around the habits that are adequate for a correct nutrition, there are always essential factors you should not leave aside so that you can take the correct choice and apply it to your lifestyle. We should therefore talk a little bit about the proteins.

The proteins are molecules that are formed by amino acids that are bonded by a type of bond known as peptide bonds. Order and disposition of amino acids depend on the genetic code of every person. Every protein is composed by: carbon, hydrogen, oxygen and nitrogen, besides from other elements such as sulfur, iron, phosphor and zinc.

Among all of the biomolecules, proteins play a fundamental part in the organism. They are essential for growth, thanks to their nitrogen contents, which is not present in other molecules, such as fat and carbon hydrates. They are also essential for the synthesis and maintenance of diverse tissues or body components, such as gastric juices, hemoglobin, vitamins, hormones and enzymes (these last act as biologic catalysts, causing an increase of the speed at which the chemical reactions of metabolism are produced). Also, they help transport certain gases through the blood, such as oxygen and carbon dioxide.

Other more specific functions are, for example, those of the antibodies, a type of proteins that act as natural defense against possible infections or external agents; collagen, which function of resistance makes it indispensable in the tissues as support, or the myosin and actin, two muscular proteins that make the movement possible, among many others. Proteins have plenty of regulating functions, since compounds such as hemoglobin, plasmatic proteins, hormones, digestive juices, enzymes and vitamins that cause the chemical reactions that happen in the organism are formed by them.

A very important function is that of resistance or structural, since proteins form support and filling tissues that give organs and tissues elasticity and resistance, such as collagen and fibrous connective tissue, and the reticuline and elastin of the elastic connective tissue.

Proteins are essentials in the diet and are present mainly in food of animal origin, such as meat, fish, eggs and milk. But they are also present in vegetal food such as soy, legumes and cereals, but in a smaller proportion. Its ingestion contributes with 4 kilocalories per gram of protein.

Proteins are nutrients that have a very big biological importance that constitute the main nutrient for the formation of muscles in the body. They are formed by amino acid chains.

There are 20 different amino acids that are combined between them in plenty of ways to form each type of proteins. Amino acids can be divided into 2 types: *essential amino acids*, which are 9, and that are obtained from food, and *non-essential amino acids*, which are 11, and are produced in our body. Given their composition and form, proteins are classified into simple or conjugated. Let's leave this aside, since the objective is not to learn about nutrition, but to use it for the purpose of the present book.

Therefore, it is necessary for us to get know the food that is rich in proteins:

Cod is a good example of a food that is rich in proteins and very low in fat, besides being an important source of vitamins and minerals that make this fish one of the foods that contain proteins that are some of the most beneficial for anyone. Also, Serrano ham contains them and its fat contents is very low.

Peanut is a nut with plenty of properties and also has a considerable amount of proteins. Every 100 grams of peanuts has 27 grams of proteins. However, when consuming it in high quantities, it alters the balance between Omega 3 and Omega 6, which has to be from 5 to 1. Also, it is hard to digest. But, in the other hand, the consumption of nuts, hazelnuts, almonds and other nuts is marvelous for many body and brain functions.

This is a small list of food rich in proteins:

> Lentils: They have around 23.5% of proteins.
> Tuna: 23% of proteins for every 100 grams of tuna.
> Peas: 23% of every 100 grams of peas is protein.
> Roquefort cheese: This is a food with 23% of proteins.
> Chicken breast: 22.8% of proteins can be found in chicken breast.
> Turkey cold cuts: This is a food that has 22.4% of proteins.
> Chorizo, cooked ham: 22% of proteins are present in these foods.
> Canned sardines: They contain 22% of proteins.
> Pork meat without fat: 21.2% of proteins.
> Goat cheese: 21% of proteins can be found in this cheese.
> Veal fillet: It delivers 20.7% of proteins.
> Lean beef: It contains 20.7% of proteins.
> Grilled chicken: 20.6% of proteins.
> Cow liver: It has 20.5% of proteins.
> Lobster, prawn, shrimp: 20.1% of proteins.
> Chickpeas: These legumes have 20% of proteins.
> Almonds: They have 20% of proteins.
> Lean pork: 20% of this type of meat is protein.

> Blood sausage: This food contains 19.5% of proteins.
> Cabrito: 19% of proteins can be found in the meat of this animal.
> White beans: These legumes contain around 19% of proteins.
> Beans: They only contain 1% of fat and 23.5% of proteins, besides of other nutrients.
> Salmon: This food contains 19% of proteins.
> Lamb: The meat of this animal contains 18% of proteins.
> Pistachios: They have 17.6% of proteins.
> Pork meat with some fat: 16.7% of this meat is protein.
> Sole fish, small hake, mackerel: These contain 16.5% of proteins.
> Snail: They have 16.3% of proteins.
> Hake: It has 15.9% of proteins.
> Pickled tuna: It contains 15% of proteins.
> Egg: It has 14% of proteins.
> Spinach: It contains 49% of proteins.
> Broccoli: It contains the astounding quantity of 45% of proteins.
> Cauliflower: It has the great quantity of 40% of proteins.
> Mushrooms: They have 38% of proteins.
> Parsley, the innocent parsley: It offers 35% of proteins.

The spinach, broccoli, cauliflower, mushrooms, parsley, chard, etc., require to be cooked in a special way or be eaten raw to keep the most proteins possible. Broccoli, cauliflower and cabbage belong to the *Cruciferae* family, which are highly recommended to fight cancer [1].

---

[1] Tip: The family called Cruciferae, mainly represented by cabbage, broccoli and cauliflower, tend, because of the cellulose they have, to cause gases when ingested. To avoid that, I recommend you to cut them in medium pieces and place them one hour in water, and take them to the pot where the water is already boiling, and leave them for 5 to 10 minutes. Then, take them out and put them in cold or iced water. By doing this, you will eliminate the annoying gases. As additional value, they will keep their

In the preceding list, I mention the proteinic value of each one of the elements, but this does not necessarily represent a recommendation, since I consider that among the readers, there are those who prefer vegetarianism or other variants.

What is described above should give you an idea of the proteinic value of plenty of foods, and it should also make you define a balanced diet, since the proteins form part of the 20% of our body weight.

Carbohydrates. They are the main source of energy of our diet. Carbohydrates, also known as saccharides, are the sugars, starch and fibers that exist in a great variety of food, such as fruits, grains, vegetables and dairy. They are composed by carbon, hydrogen and oxygen; the body cannot fabricate them by itself, and therefore should be provided through food. Carbohydrates provide body with glucose, which is transformed into energy, which is used to keep the bodily functions and physical activity.

The healthiest sources of carbohydrates are the unprocessed, or minimally processed foods, such as whole grains, vegetables, fruits and grains.

The less healthy sources include white bread, cakes, sugared sodas and other foods that are highly processed or refined.

There are three main types of carbohydrates:

Sugar: This is the simplest for of carbohydrates. It is naturally produced in some foods, including fruits, vegetables, milk and dairy. Sugars include sugar from the fruit (fructose), table sugar (sucrose) and sugar from the milk (lactose).

Starch: This is a complex carbohydrate, which means that is formed by many units of sugar linked together. Starch is naturally produced in vegetables, grains, cooked beans and peas.

Fiber: The fiber is also a complex carbohydrate, which is

bright color and will stay crispy, just the way they are supposed to be eaten.

naturally produced in fruits, vegetables, whole grains, cooked beans and peas.

I mentioned that carbohydrates produce the fuel for the central nervous system and the energy for the muscles, but they also avoid the proteins and fat to be used as source of energy.

The carbohydrates we should consume should have the following characteristics: low or moderate in fat, with enough nutrients, without sugars or refined grains, with high contents of natural fiber, low in sodium, saturated fat and trans fat. Trans fat are those that have been hydrogenated and are present in fried potato chips, cookies, margarines and some snacks manufactured with vegetable oil. As an example, I will share the following list:

Fried potato chips (150g): 7gr of trans fat.

Hamburger (200gr): 3gr of trans fat.

Madeleines (1 unit): 1-2.1gr of trans fat.

Cookies (2 units): 1.3gr of trans fat.

Margarine (1 tablespoon): 0.9gr of trans fat.

Cereal bar (1 unit): 0.4 of trans fat.

Chocolate bar (80gr): 0.75gr of trans fat.

What do you have for breakfast? What snacks do you eat in your get-togethers? What do you use to prepare them?

Refined sugar and starch are the direct cause of the increase in low density cholesterol, or the "bad" one, such as the formation of atheromatous plaques in the main arteries of the body, and the coronary arteries as well, which are the ones that feed the heart muscle.

Also, they lead to the development of diabetes, obesity, decrease in the *brain derived neurotrophic factor* (BDNF). This means that they notoriously affect the brain functions due to the way they affect the production and usage of this factor. I wonder how they affect in the so-called demential diseases.

Even though the carbohydrates are certainly the main source of energy of our body, when notoriously decreasing it, fat will automatically be taken as source of energy, which will help in maintaining an ideal weight; however, it could lead to *ketosis* when the descent in the carbohydrates is very important. If the decrease in saccharides continues, our body takes the proteins from the muscular mass, causing *sarcopenia*, or the decrease of the muscular mass to be used as energy, which is not at all convenient.

Now, the sudden decrease in the carbohydrates affects our energy and the correct functioning of our brain, and that is why in moments of *hypoglycemia* we could even lose consciousness.

The advisable thing to do is decreasing the carbohydrates in a precise and directed way, and if considered convenient, limit them to the point where you can lose weight using fat as source of energy.

Next, I will show you some real data that you will surely find interesting and maybe even amazing:

Presently, an average individual eats an average of 61 kgs of sugar. Only 9% of the population eat the 5 recommended portions of fruits and vegetables that are rich in vitamins.

An incredible 80% of the carbohydrates that are consumed are in the shape of refined flours and sugars.

Millions of people eat 230 calories more per day than just 15 years ago. Our daily diet consists in foods that are very processed or refined. The increase in the consumption of food that is low in nutrients means that we have an even higher demand of vitamins and minerals that are needed to be able to metabolize them.

Almost all the foods have pesticides, chemical dioxins and fluorides that enter our body every day. It has been proven that most of the hamburgers that are served in fast food restaurants contain traces of more than 100 pesticides.

Most of the meats have residues of antibiotics, hormones and chemical leftovers that have toxic effects on our bodies.

Our food is contaminated with residues of the containers such as plastic, polystyrene (Styrofoam), Tupperware and Teflon in the frying pans that go into our system.

Even the common practice of using plastic containers in the microwave contaminates our food with toxins.

More than 10% of the calories that are consumed in Mexico come from alcoholic beverages. Alcohol in big quantities damages the liver, and this decreases vitamin B, zinc and magnesium.

Medical prescriptions and unprescribed medicines can decrease the nutrients.

Those who exercise regularly have a significantly higher need of anti-oxidants and minerals.

In the present days, millions of people follow a diet and need supplements just to fulfill their minimal nutritional demands. Diets increase the production of free radicals, which is why more anti-oxidants are needed to decrease the damage done to the liver and other organs that sometimes happens during weight loss.

In preceding paragraphs, I mentioned eliminating from your diet the five whites, and one of them is the refined sugars. To refresh that comment a little bit, I will mention the other four: milk's cow, refined flours, mined salt and white rice. There are plenty of nutritionists that call sugar "the white poison", and I totally agree.

Now, what proportion of carbohydrates do we need daily?

As I was mentioning earlier, carbohydrates are the primary source of energy, fuel for the brain functions and all of our organs, however, when you ingest a portion that is greater than the one your body needs, this turns into body fat, which translates into weight increase.

It has been determined by merely medical sources that the amount of carbohydrates that our body needs is from 45 to 60% of the total daily ingestion of calories. A gram of their molecules gives 4 calories to the body.

Carbohydrates can be one of two kinds: simples, as sucrose and lactose, which means that they are the ones that provide the sweet flavor to food and that are quickly absorbed, and the other kind of carbohydrates are the complex ones, which means that are composed by long sugar chains, which are slowly absorbed in the organism. These are found in bread, tortillas, oat, beans, fava beans, lentils and whole grain cereals.

Even fiber is part of the carbohydrates because it is constituted by linked units of sugar; fruits, vegetables and whole grains are examples of fiber.

Therefore, it is very advisable to eat small amounts of complex carbohydrates and increase those in fruits and vegetables.

I do not want to move forward without mentioning the 10 foods that will definitely give you a life with a better quality if you consume them frequently, alone or accompanying your main dishes and salads: **beetroot**, raw in salads, in juice, as it contains vitamin C, iron, magnesium and potassium; **asparagus**, marvelous food with vitamin A, potassium and proteins; **sweet potato**, which contains beta-carotenes, vitamins A, C and K, besides fiber; **quinoa**, which is one of the seeds I mentioned before, and that contains proteins, fiber, amino acids, iron, magnesium and copper; **beans**, rich in iron, zinc and vitamins; **broccoli**, which I already mentioned that belongs to the Cruciferae. Besides the vitamins, this is another food that fights cancer, as it nourishes the production of stem cells; **cranberries**, containers of potassium, anti-oxidants and vitamin C, in shakes or directly to the mouth, they reduce the frequency of the heart diseases; **avocado**, a delicious source of potassium, calcium, vitamin E and proteins; its type of fat improves the quality of your skin; **garlic**, which contains anti-oxidants, selenium, vitamins C and B6, besides from magnesium; and finally, **green tea**, which given its great amount of anti-oxidants, prevents heart attacks, reduces cholesterol and improves your metabolism.

Something very important: I have certainly mentioned the need of nourishing yourself with fruits, vegetables, meat, fish, nuts, etc., however, I must remind you that the nutritional elements that 20-40 years ago were contained in the fruits and vegetables, especially, ARE NOT the amounts that they currently contain: to obtain the nutritious elements that the apple contains, you would have to eat from 7 to 10 apples nowadays (please look for organic products). The nutrients that 1 kilo of tomatoes contain were contained in only a pair of those many years ago, and this happens with every fruit and vegetable, because of the factors in which they are sowed, watered, grown, harvested and kept until they reach your table, and therefore, it is very advisable and convenient to complement your daily diet with nutritional supplements (I don't know why they're called like that: supplements, since, from my limited point of view, the term in Spanish refers to substitution, and I consider that they complement it, but anyway, let's continue to use the terms that the experts use, as the should use them for some reason I don't completely understand). As I was saying, those nutritional supplements are necessary, on one hand, because they are already processed, and if I recommend powdered curcuma, there are companies that sell *curcumin*, which is the active part of curcuma, contained in capsules, just the same as the Mexican thistle, the vitamins, all of the vitamins! There are dozens of companies that distribute these nutritional supplements through multi-level systems, and this is why they lose credibility sometimes. However, there are plenty of companies that faithfully adhere to placing in their products the needed nutrients to fulfill their objective. Do some research or ask me. I will gladly tell you which are the companies I trust, even though they distribute their products through the same method.

I will soon be able to offer you supplements based on ayurvedic medicine, which in my opinion are extraordinarily beneficial, and at fair prices.

CONCLUSION

As I have insisted, this is not a treaty on nutrition, or medical measures to cure the diseases of the world and its inhabitants. My sole objective is to make you more aware of what from very early age you should consider AND practice to help you avoid living your old age disgracefully, depending on others, filled with ailments, frustrations, "what ifs" and what is worse... really old.

You should naturally apply every point that has been mentioned, especially those related to health and diet, as they are very closely related.

In this part, I pretend, in very few words, to gather all of the information I have placed in this, your book, and in an agile, precise, concise way, share the decisions I have taken to suggest to my patients while seeking a better quality of life in every sense. During the elaboration of this work I have passed many hours reading especially about the nutritional aspect, the diets that the maximum authorities of the matter in the whole world, and of course, in Mexico, suggest; also, more hours analyzing the advises that many, many medicine professionals consider healthy, as well as advises that "should" be followed every day to obtain what they consider a healthy life.

I have read that the hands should NOT be washed with soaps that contain cracks, as plenty of bacteria lives there. I wonder, if the soaps are supposed to be bacteria killers, then why the hell do they even exist? Others say that anti-bacterial gels should not be used, since they cause adverse effects to the skin; there is someone else around there that indicates the proper way to get into the shower, so that you don't have negative effects. In other words, he indicates which part of your body you should get wet first, and which one should follow. I definitely believe that in this field, there is us, a bunch of wackos that want to spread concepts that are healthy in every way, and some that fall (and please note that I said "fall") in the ridiculous, obsessive and even totally fake things. There are "experts" (when Albert Einstein was introduced as an "expert in physics", he said: life is too short to be an expert in something. I am only a lover of physics")... ok, I stand corrected: there are those who call themselves experts in nutrition and the only thing they achieve is to create neurosis in the every day life, from the moment we get up of our beds to the moment we go back to them, and the position we sleep in: the darned toothpaste has, according to them, carcinogen agents and other damaging contents; according to them, you should clean your teeth with ashes from a burnt tortilla. Yes! They are right! But can you imagine the ritual when washing your teeth? PLEASE DO NOT FILL YOUR LIFE AND YOUR MIND of so much bullshit! You are more than you think or suppose you are, based in this bunch of concepts. Yes, they may be entirely right! But please, if you fill your mind with all these things, you might as well live in a crystal bubble in a totally sterile environment, receiving your meals through a purifying system based on all kinds of science, and the day even you think on going out to... fart outside that bubble, you could be the perfect prey of all of the damaging elements that exist in the world, and you might even die in two or three minutes... Absurd!

In my childhood (what I really did in that stage was look after my brothers, since we were 11 and I am the oldest), we lived in the neighborhood of Sagrada Familia in Guadalajara. In the Juan N. Cumplido street there were plenty of neighborhoods, and the children that lived there ran around half-naked, with green snot coming out of their noses, some fell down and broke an arm, some others were ran over by a car, and came up just fine from those situations. We lived with certain comforts and medical care, but always, ALWAYS were taking medicines, as my beautiful mother considered that we needed to be on treatments at all time, for every disease.

The children of the street I mentioned never really got sick, (with the exception of the green snot). They used their dirty hands to take to their mouth anything they found on the floor. Now I wonder, what was the factor that kept them healthy, and us, despite of my mother's cares, sick? That they did not consider that the sickness was caused by their habits, of course, since their mothers were cooking, doing somebody else's laundry, cleaning somebody else's house for some money, some even selling their body, others pregnant and controlling the alcoholic husband. What I want to say is that the concept of sickness DID NOT exist, as they were *distracted* in living life the best way they could.

Facundo Cabral wrote, recorded and sang in his book "You are not Depressed, you are Distracted" these solid concepts: *you give more importance to the fatal things you listen to than to the beauty you are as human being. You speak more of the negative things than of the positive things; you give more attention to the painful things that happen every day than to the marvel life is...* this makes me think and remember that during that afternoon we spent together, we decreed that us good people are more than bad people... that there is more kindness and health in us than the culture of disease that has been sowed in us since so long.

I also have the absolute conviction in what Dr. Bruce Lipton quotes in his book "The Biology of Belief", where he states that what I have mentioned in plenty of moments is absolutely and unmistakably true. This excellent human being, investigator, speaker throughout the world, even states, with proven scientific foundations that genes DO NOT manage our life, or its quality; we can be the ones who manage it; therefore, those "diseases" that are said to have genetic origins, or that are inherited, could perfectly be healed or not even activated, using our positive thoughts, emotions and some exercises through which we will free ourselves from the heavy burden represented by the conviction that many, many diseases are product of hereditary factors for which we cannot do nothing to cure them, but only improve the quality of life.

Thinking a little bit more, I remembered that there are those who unmistakably state that there is an "alcoholism gen" (...) in such a way that if you have it you are condemned to suffer from alcoholism, since it is a disease: great, isn't it? Do you really think this is possible? That alcoholism is a disease? In my personal conviction, any addiction is a choice, but never a disease.

Given the above, I want to sow in you the courage to understand that anything that may come in a negative way that may affect you or pretend to affect you could be defeated even before beginning, as long as you understand and accept that the most powerful principle to avoid, prevent and even heal is within yourself.

I have shared with you some of the things I have learned throughout many years of an open attitude, not tied any more by the medicine that excited me since I can remember, the changes I have lived with the intention to help as much as I can every human being that approaches me asking for orientation for their diseases or hard situations in their life, and after all of this, I have come to the conclusion that any disease will put down its roots in you once you give it a place and credibility in your life. The greatest power that exists in this Universe, or Multiverse, as many say now, humbly lies within you, waiting for you to give it the value to make you powerful and immune to any condition or disease, and that has been despised or ignored because what surrounds us every day leads us to create dependencies with external things to alleviate or cure what we call diseases. The modeling of your body, your life, your day to day with a convincing decision based on the information that I have given to you, and in the absolute faith that you are a superior being, and that the quality of life you have depends in you, will make me feel like I have achieved the purpose by writing this book.

You are a being that is infinitely superior to what you can imagine: centuries and centuries of evolution have brought you to this moment of your life, and therefore, you are not *just somebody else in the world*, but a being with so much power and ability that when activating them can achieve whatever you set your mind to. Remember that you are the product of your thoughts, and that it is your commitment to yourself creating thoughts that are loyal to a worthy, happy and intense life that is filled with energy, that learns from the blows and the falls, since they are given precisely for that: learn, evolve and transcend. We were born to innovate, since loving is creating, creating is growing, and growing is making those that surrounds us grow. This way, we will bequeath an absolutely beautiful image to our successors.

The description of the 12 points that in my point of view, take you to the quality of life in the old age are not started in the old age, but during childhood, stage in which anything that is sowed will yield fruits, regardless of the seed that is sowed. This is why it is the responsibility of the parents and especially of the grandparents *preventing*, and from early stages of life, and during the rest of the life of our children or grandchildren, encourage the exercise of these 12 points according to their comprehension and age, so that real *gerontoprophylaxis* can exist. In this way, there will be many, many longstanding human beings without any real ailment; only those who are "paying the excesses of their youth in their old age".

IINDEX

PROLOGUE	5
DEDICATION	15
INTRODUCTION	17
CLARIFICATION	21

FIRST PART

SENSE OF BELONGING	25
IDENTITY	35
GOALS	41
MATERIAL POSSESSIONS	47
SOCIALIZATION	55
AFFECTIVITY	61
SEXUALITY	67
SPIRITUALITY	75
AUTONOMY	81

SECOND PART

MY FIVE WISHES	89
ANTICIPATED WILL DOCUMENT	95
PERSONAL CONCEPTS REGARDING THE ATTENTION OF TERMINALLY ILL AND THE RIGHTS THEY BEAR	103
HEALTH	109
THE DISEASE	133
ALTERNATIVE MEDICINES	151

THIRD PART

NUTRITION	163
CONCLUSION	185
INDEX	191

MY OLD AGE, A MENU I MUST CHOOSE
se terminó de imprimir en marzo de 2019
Salió de la imprenta de ae Ediciones al cuidado de Alberto Escobar
Emilio Carranza Nº 1353-8, col. El Vigía, Zapopan, Jalisco
Teléfono (33) 3640-2128 contacto@aeediciones.com
Tiraje: 100 ejemplares

Diseño de portada:
Alberto Escobar